"Don't you *dare* do that again!"

Whitney struck Gabe's hand away, refusing his attempt to steady her when she lost her footing.

Anger mingled with disgust on his face. "Don't *dare?*" he drawled, mocking her righteous tone. "You mean, 'Keep my place,' don't you? Not to try anything with my betters?"

Whitney tossed her head back. "Interpret it any way you want," she said from between clenched teeth. "Just because we're stuck out here in the wilderness doesn't mean I want to play 'You Tarzan, Me Jane.' Keep that in mind—and that's an *order.*"

"Who gives the orders around here may become an interesting matter before all this is over," he challenged softly.

And for one brief moment, the thought of taking orders—Gabe's orders—and of leaning on someone else's strength besides her own, sounded very appealing to Whitney.

Bethany Campbell, an English major and textbook consultant, calls her writing world her ''hidey-hole,'' that marvelous place where true love always wins out. Her hobbies include writing poetry and thinking about that little scar on Harrison Ford's chin. She laughingly admits that her husband, who produces videos and writes comedy, approves of the first one only.

Bethany received the 1990 Maggie Award for her Harlequin Romance #3062 *Dancing Sky*. It's just one of this talented author's many romances to have delighted readers around the world.

Books by Bethany Campbell

HARLEQUIN ROMANCE

3062—DANCING SKY
3079—THE ENDS OF THE EARTH
3109—EVERY WOMAN'S DREAM
3133—THE CLOUD HOLDERS
3163—EVERY KIND OF HEAVEN
3187—SPELLBINDER

HARLEQUIN INTRIGUE

65—PROS AND CONS
116—THE ROSE OF CONSTANT
151—DEAD OPPOSITES

SAND DOLLAR

Bethany Campbell

Harlequin Books

TORONTO • NEW YORK • LONDON
AMSTERDAM • PARIS • SYDNEY • HAMBURG
STOCKHOLM • ATHENS • TOKYO • MILAN
MADRID • WARSAW • BUDAPEST • AUCKLAND

ISBN 0-373-03211-0

Harlequin Romance first edition August 1992

SAND DOLLAR

CHAPTER ONE

SHE DIDN'T LIKE his looks.

He was the "captain" for the trip, and he stood silhouetted against the gray sea, watching her board the yacht. He also watched the two men with her, but most of his attention, deceptively lazy, was focused on her.

His look was one of brash appraisal, too bold and hungry for comfort. She recognized it and hated it.

He was handsome in a rough, careless way, and he might as well have had the word "rebel" branded across his forehead. He hadn't shaved for two or three days, and his jaw and upper lip glittered with dark gold stubble. His sunstreaked hair fell, wind-tossed, over his forehead.

His black-and-white Hawaiian shirt was unbuttoned and whipped in the breeze, revealing a broad and bronzed golden-haired chest. His white shorts rode low on his lean hips, and he wore no socks with his battered deck shoes.

He looked like the sort who lived for the moment, who drifted aimlessly wherever chance took him. He was, in short, the kind of man she'd left behind her long ago—the kind of man she never wanted to deal with again. He made her old defenses spring back to uneasy life, warning her. She was a disciplined woman, but for a moment, he took her back across the years, and her heart pitched more wildly than the waves of the Atlantic that tossed behind him.

Trouble, said all her instincts and training. *Easy,* said her logic. *His kind can't hurt you now.*

Logic won. She was nervous, she told herself, only because of the importance of today's mission. She raised her chin a trifle higher, breathed in the crisp October air and acted as if the blond man were invisible to her.

But still, his presence thrust itself into her consciousness. Out of the corner of her eye, she watched him as carefully as he watched her.

No, she didn't like his looks at all.

And from the way he twisted his mouth, Whitney thought, she pleased him no better than he did her. His bronzed brows had a permanent downward slant at their inner corners, his eyes a permanent narrowing that gave him a wry, critical expression.

"Our captain, Gabe Cantrell, I take it," said Mr. Mortalwood, offering his hand to the man. "I'm Lawrence Mortalwood. The owner."

Cantrell shook hands, then leaned against the rail so casually that Whitney found his manner bordering dangerously on disrespectful.

"Cantrell, these are my guests, Miss Whitney Shane and Mr. Adrian Fisk. Miss Shane and Mr. Fisk, Gabe Cantrell, our captain."

Cantrell nodded, his eyes slitted against the sun, his mouth crooked as if in private amusement. His glance had flicked idly over the elderly Mr. Mortalwood, resplendent in yachting clothes so new that his white shoes did not have the smallest of scuffs.

Cantrell's gaze skimmed Adrian Fisk with the same dismissiveness. Laconically he offered Fisk his hand. Adrian, who was tidy and dark and quick to sense any sort of slight, made the handshake as brief as possible. He didn't smile at Cantrell, and Cantrell didn't seem to mind.

Cantrell's eyes turned to Whitney and there they lingered. He seemed to take in every detail of her appearance and, with inexplicable insolence, to find it a source of mirth.

"*Miss* Shane," he said, cocking one eyebrow. He reached for her leather garment bag. "May I stow that for you?"

Whitney, keeping tight hold of the garment bag, as well as her briefcase, turned from him and stared out at the harbor. The sea was steely today, and to the north, gulls dipped and swooped over the green grasses of the marsh.

"No. I'll be going below to change," she said coolly.

"Good idea," said Cantrell. He had a slow, languid voice, more Western than Southern, that put an ironic spin on his words.

She made a point not to make eye contact with him. She knew that at the moment she looked out of place on the yacht. Her story at the office had been that she was attending a client's wedding and reception. She wore her dark gold-colored silk suit, the matching snakeskin pumps, and a white silk blouse.

Mr. Mortalwood liked her to wear silk blouses—he thought them both businesslike and feminine—so she did whenever it was appropriate, because it was important to Whitney that she please Mr. Mortalwood.

"I'll show you to your stateroom, Whitney," said Mr. Mortalwood briskly. Taking the garment bag from her, he left his own bag on deck for Cantrell to carry. Mortalwood placed his other hand paternally on Whitney's arm and guided her down a tiny flight of stairs. She could feel Cantrell watching them.

"I'm sorry things aren't in better shape," Mr. Mortalwood said, opening a door that needed refinishing. The small stateroom smelled musty, and the plaid curtains and bedspreads had a limp, faded air.

"I haven't had this thing out for three years," Mortalwood said, regret in his voice. "Not since Lila...got ill. I should refurbish everything. Ah, how she loved this boat."

Sorrow tinged his tone. Lawrence Mortalwood's wife had died eleven months ago. She had been an elegant, witty woman, as deeply involved in the real-estate and development business as her husband, and Whitney had both respected and liked her. In turn, Lila Mortalwood had taken Whitney under her wing.

Whitney knew some people in the company had resented her friendship with Lila, but she hadn't cared. She had truly liked the woman and been inspired by her. There were some who said Lila had been the moral and business force behind the Mortalwood Corporation, and Whitney had greatly admired her.

"I'll have to do something," Mr. Mortalwood muttered, shaking his head. "She'd hate to see it like this. You know Lila. Everything had to be just so. *You* remember."

Whitney smiled. She remembered well; Lila Mortalwood had been a perfectionist. She would have hated the layer of dust on the stateroom's furniture and the smell of mildew hovering in the air. The scent reminded Whitney of the house by the river where she'd lived with her grandmother and uncle years ago. Her smile faded.

Recalling the past made her remember the quietly insolent man on the deck, and she couldn't resist the impulse to express her displeasure with him. "Your captain—shouldn't he have seen to everything? He seems lackadaisical."

"Cantrell? He's temporary, Whitney. He hadn't been aboard the boat himself before this morning. I let my other captain go when Lila got so... when we couldn't make it to the coast...she missed it. How she missed it...." His voice trailed off, distracted. He looked about the stateroom unhappily.

Mortalwood shook his head again. "The people at the marina were *supposed* to keep it up. They did, on the outside. But they've neglected the interior. It's shameful." He gave another sigh. "But it'll be good to get her out to sea again. *Lila's Little Darling,*" he said, reciting the yacht's name as if it could somehow invoke the lost Lila.

He turned, smiling at Whitney indulgently. He was not a handsome man, but his harsh features could sometimes look kindly. "Don't worry about our captain—he works only long enough to get us to Sand Dollar, then Hilton Head, then back. He'll know nothing. He doesn't even know that Sand Dollar's our first stop."

"You're lucky he's temporary," Whitney said, setting her briefcase and purse on one of the twin bunks. "He strikes me as disrespectful. You're sure you can trust him?"

Mortalwood smiled slyly. "He's new in town, and he shouldn't have the foggiest notion of who we are, where we're from or what we're up to. I made it clear when I had him hired that he wasn't to know."

He took off his yachting cap and stroked his thinning white hair. "He thinks we're taking the boat out to see how seaworthy she is. That I'm deciding whether to keep her. I'll tell him we're stopping at Sand Dollar Island just to drop anchor somewhere. Take a look, have a picnic lunch, go on to Hilton Head. Don't worry—he'll never be on the payroll again. Particularly if you disapprove of him. After all, you're my management specialist."

Whitney nodded, pleased. She had influence with Mr. Mortalwood, or Mr. M., as he let privileged employees such as she call him. She didn't hesitate to use her influence when it was for his own good, and staying clear of a person like Cantrell, she'd decided, would be to *anyone's* good.

Let the man, his stubble, his unbuttoned shirt and equally unbuttoned manners drift out of their lives as quickly as possible. He obviously didn't mix well with a group of respectable, hardworking people, people with *real* business to do. And today, Whitney, Mr. M. and Adrian Fisk *had* important business.

"I'll leave you here to change," Mr. M. said, setting her garment bag on the bunk. He was a small man, no taller than Whitney, but he had grown heavier since his wife's death. He'd had to buy new clothes, larger ones for this outing, and he looked oddly incongruous in his spanking white shoes and slacks, his blue blazer and white yachting cap.

He seemed, Whitney thought sympathetically, like a man in a costume, playing a part. He was too short, pale and bulky to look like an outdoorsman. In addition, he was still getting used to his new trifocals, so that lately he was always craning his head at experimental angles, like a stout, uncomfortable bird.

He gave her a rather mechanical smile and stepped from her room, closing the door. He really hadn't seemed himself since Lila had died, Whitney thought with concern; Sand Dollar Island was the first project that had stirred him out of his sorrow. She heard his slow steps lumbering away, and then the roar of the yacht's starting engine drowned them out.

Lawrence Mortalwood was getting old and he was showing it, she realized regretfully. He and Lila had been her mentors, back when Whitney had been one of the youngest and greenest of real-estate agents in his chain of companies based in Atlanta, Georgia. Lila had noticed Whitney's sales record and picked her for the management-training program, where Whitney had concentrated all her energies into excelling.

Now she was one of four vice presidents at the Mortalwood Corporation, in charge of management. Chances were excellent that soon she would be promoted to executive vice president. It grew increasingly likely that when Lawrence Mortalwood retired, he would select her to replace him as the chief executive officer of the company.

Adrian Fisk was her greatest rival for these choice positions, but she knew, quite honestly, that Mr. Mortalwood didn't *like* Adrian as much as he liked her.

Adrian had one permanent and unmendable flaw. He lacked charm; his personality had a hard, unpleasant edge. Mr. Mortalwood was simply more comfortable working with Whitney, just as he had always been with Lila, who knew how to keep his eccentricities and insecurities tactfully on even keel.

Whitney had worked extraordinarily hard, but she had been lucky, as well, and for this she was sincerely grateful. She was a Cinderella, and she knew it.

"Golden Girl," she'd heard a secretary call her once, envy vibrating in the woman's voice. "A charmed life," somebody else had said of her, and it was true.

But none of them knew how much of a Cinderella she really was, or how charmed her life had actually been. That suited Whitney fine, for the less people knew about her past, the better.

She had severed herself from that past, risen far from her roots, and with her mother's help, she had painstakingly recreated herself from what she had once been. What she had been was a poor child with no father and bad grammar, living just outside an ugly little town that smelled night and day with the stink of paper mills.

Yes, she thought, slipping out of the silk suit, she'd come farther than she'd ever dreamed, farther even than her mother had dreamed. She wished her mother were alive to see her now, a vice president—and still on her way up—at only twenty-seven years old.

She hung her suit and blouse in the slightly dank closet. Mr. M. really was going to have to do something about this yacht, Whitney thought; now that she'd seen it, she must remind him how sad its state was. That was one of her unofficial jobs now that Lila was gone: she had to keep Mr. Mortalwood's life in order.

Whitney pulled on a pair of navy blue slacks—she would not wear shorts, even though October in Georgia could be warm. Mr. M. didn't approve of young women who showed too much leg, especially young women in his employ. She added an expensive long-sleeved green sweater trimmed with navy at the cuffs and neckline and then tied the sleeves of a matching cardigan about her neck so it hung like a light cape around her shoulders.

She looked into a smudged mirror and smoothed her blond hair, although it didn't need smoothing. She wore it pulled back softly, not severely, and tucked into a French twist. It was as neatly trained as the mind that functioned so efficiently beneath it.

She touched up her makeup, which she kept minimal. The barest hint of gray shadow to highlight her blue-gray eyes, simple bright red on her full lips.

There, she thought with a toss of her head. Now she looked appropriately dressed for a day on the yacht. Let that unshaven captain with his narrowed, critical, mocking eyes smirk at her *now*.

Whitney turned from the mirror, instructing herself to ignore—what was his name?—Cantrell as coolly and politely as possible for the rest of the trip. He was a temporary and unimportant irritant.

She had more pressing matters than Cantrell on her mind. Together she, Mr. M., and Fisk would decide whether to make the boldest move in the Mortalwood Corporation's history. They had a chance to buy—covertly—one of Georgia's last available tidal barrier islands, the farthest flung and least developed one, Sand Dollar.

Fisk had set up the deal with annoying secrecy, which worried Whitney. It meant he was trying to keep Whitney in the dark and to curry favor with Mr. M.; she wouldn't put it past him.

But Mr. M. wanted Whitney's opinions about Sand Dollar and said he would make no decision without her. Seizing Sand Dollar, Mr. M. said repeatedly, could turn out to be the biggest piece of wheeling and dealing in Georgia real estate in this decade. And she, Whitney Shane, once the fatherless little kid from the mill town, was one of the chief wheelers and dealers.

Once again, with a pang, she wished her mother could see her now. She'd be more excited than Whitney herself, who, shutting the door behind her, almost ran up the stairs, eager to join Mr. M.

On deck, she nearly collided with Gabe Cantrell as he strolled from the tiny upper galley, a tray of drinks in his hand.

"Damn!" he said, swerving to avoid her. A martini splashed over the edge of its glass. "Where's the fire? On a boat, you're supposed to relax."

He startled her, and she had come so close to bumping into him that her arm had brushed his bare chest. She had drawn it back as if singed.

Drat! Whitney thought with vehemence. She realized one of the things she disliked was his sheer physicality. She had grown used to men who were creatures of the intellect and knowledge, men who sat behind desks most of the day.

This man reminded her of the roughly handsome men back in Kanker County. When they were young, such men had a harsh male beauty. But then the poverty of the town, the work and the stench of the mill broke them down, made them into dull-eyed animals. They were nothing and they had nothing to offer their women. She wanted to stay away from such men for the rest of her life.

Cantrell narrowed his eyes, and the fine lines at their outer edges deepened. His mouth curled snidely up at one corner. Under the stubble he had dimples, deep and almost groovelike. Whitney narrowed her own eyes as she realized the man was silently laughing at her.

Enough was enough. He needed to be put in his place. "You've spilled Mr. Mortalwood's martini," she said coolly. "Please make another. And he likes an onion in it, not an olive. Weren't you supposed to see that the bar was properly stocked? And don't bruise the gin, or I'll have to remake it myself."

The dimples disappeared. "Maybe you'd better make it right yourself—Miss Shane. I flunked bartending school."

You probably flunked every school you were ever in, Whitney thought uncharitably. "Give me this," she said, her voice clipped, taking the tray. "Watch me do it, and try to get it right."

"Yes, ma'am," he said with mock obedience. He followed her into the narrow confines of the galley, where he stood too close to her side. She was certain he did it on purpose, just to be annoying. She felt the heat of his tall, sun-drenched body and wished he'd button his shirt.

Trying to ignore him, she opened the small refrigerator. "These," she said, brandishing the jar, "are cocktail onions. They're what Mr. Mortalwood prefers—speared through half way, not completely—with a plastic toothpick, preferably blue."

She looked about irritably for the toothpicks and saw the box lying open on the counter. They were all plain wooden toothpicks, not a blue one in the lot. "This bar hasn't been stocked properly," Whitney said, her voice icy as a displeased queen's. "Now I *know* that Mr. Mortalwood's secretary gave you complete instructions because I personally reminded—"

"Nobody told me to color-coordinate the toothpicks." If her tone was ice, Gabe Cantrell's was fire. It clearly warned that he didn't take criticism meekly. He was probably the sort of man who couldn't stand having a woman as his superior. It would stick in his craw so much he'd fight her all the way.

Well, she thought, she'd have to teach him better tolerance. She kept her face blank, tossed him a brief, frosty glance and tried to open the bottle of onions.

The top wouldn't budge. She tried again, until she was forced almost to grimace with the effort. He watched her, his face as blank and rigid as her own.

She rapped the edge of the cap on the counter to loosen it. It wouldn't budge.

"May I be of assistance?" he almost hissed. He still stood too close and his breath hotly tingled her ear. He took the bottle, his hand brushing hers, and she started at its roughness. She was used to men with hands almost as smooth as her own. His were lean and powerful, marked by innumerable scars and tough with calluses.

"It's easy," he said, twisting the lid off effortlessly, "if you know how." He handed the jar back to her and leaned against the counter, his shirt opening to reveal more of his well-toned body. To her surprise she saw he had a blue tattoo on his right pectoral muscle right over his heart. It was a small picture of an extremely evil-looking alligator. The alligator was grinning.

Quickly she turned her gaze away, embarrassed by the sight of the tattoo. "Sometimes," she said, plucking out an onion, "brains must bow to brawn. Thank you."

"Yes," he said stonily. "Sometimes brains have to absolutely grovel to brawn. You're welcome."

"Watch," she said, ignoring his gibe. "The onion is half-pierced by the toothpick." She illustrated, carefully inserting the toothpick into the onion's translucent skin. She lay it down neatly on a cocktail napkin.

"Fascinating," he said out of the side of his mouth. He folded his arms across his chest, a gesture of boredom. Although he didn't quite smile, his groovelike dimples played again.

His posture, leaning against the cabinet, was casual; so was his voice and so was the careless, smirking set of his mouth. But his eyes, dark gray and half-veiled by bronze lashes, were disconcertingly alert. They gleamed with intelligence she hadn't expected and found somehow threatening.

"Where's the martini shaker?" she asked shortly.

"Right behind me," he said with a shrug. He made no effort to reach for it.

She refused to give him the satisfaction of asking for it. She had won wars of willpower with better men than he would ever be. Keeping her eyes trained unflinchingly on his, she reached behind him, groping for the shaker. Her sweatered arm brushed his hard, bare one, but he didn't move away.

At that moment, the yacht bucked like a horse and she was thrown against his chest. To steady her, he caught her in one arm with a movement so swift it startled her. She gasped.

The yacht pitched again, this time in the opposite direction. Gabe pulled Whitney more tightly against him to keep her from being tossed the other way.

In surprise, her heart lurched almost as violently as the boat. Her face accidentally pressed against the muscled warmth of his chest and was tickled by the curling golden hairs. He had instinctively straightened when the boat dipped and plummeted, and she hadn't realized until that moment how tall he was or how strong.

Whitney tried to regain her balance and pull away from him, but the boat seemed to skip up in the air, then land hard, slapping the water. She shuddered, squeezing her eyes shut and flinching against him.

He clutched her more firmly and swore. She heard the word rumble deep in his chest when he said it. Involuntarily she curled her hands into fists and realized she was huddling against him, intuitively accepting his protection.

Then the boat's path seemed to even out, but she kept her eyes shut, expecting another jolt. His arm stayed around her, tensed, waiting. He swore again.

Whitney clenched her teeth, anticipating for the space of one heartbeat, two, three. Nothing happened, except that instinctively she stayed next to him, and he held her fast.

His heartbeat was beneath her ear, strong and swift. He exuded the clean scent of sun-warmed flesh and the sea wind in autumn. Something tingled against her lips and she knew it was the crisp hair of his chest.

She grew more conscious of the arm wrapped so firmly around her and became aware that his other hand rested almost possessively on her shoulder. She felt the steady rise and fall of his breathing and realized something warm prickled intriguingly at her ear. It was his stubbled jaw, resting against her hair.

Slightly dazed, she was startled by his voice, harsh and intimately close. "Are you all right?" He made no move to release her, and when he spoke his jaw scratched, not unpleasantly, against her ear.

For the length of another pair of heartbeats she said nothing. She'd never been held as tightly by a man; she never would have allowed it under ordinary circumstances.

Chagrined, she pulled away. There was a calculating and self-satisfied look in his eyes and a quizzical smile on his lips that she didn't like. The galley felt smaller than before, and the air between them seemed to throb ominously.

The drinks had spilled, the onion had rolled off the tray, and the toothpicks had flown out of the box and now littered the counter. The martini shaker, tipped onto its side, had rolled into the corner of the counter.

All these troubling details imprinted themselves on her consciousness. But what she was most aware of was how her flesh tingled where he had touched her. "I'm fine," she said, straightening the sweater that hung about her shoulders.

"Yes," he said ambiguously. "You are." The smile kept playing at the corners of his mouth, and his eyes, with their same intent and calculating look, contemplated her lips.

"What a mess," Whitney said, perturbed. She glowered about the galley, because he not only seemed to enjoy the situation, but enjoy it too much. "What happened? Shouldn't you be piloting this boat, or whatever you do?"

He nodded and set the martini shaker upright. "Yes. I should. But your friend, Mr. Whistlewood or Mr. Milkweed or whoever, wanted to take the wheel. I was demoted to steward."

He gave her a mock salute. "I was just standing here taking orders, trying to learn to build a better martini."

Whitney was not amused. She emptied the drinks into the small sink. "Well," she said with elaborate calm, "I suggest you see if Mr. Mortalwood wants you to take over the wheel again. It's been a while since he's been on the boat, and he's not used to his new glasses yet. Some supervision might be in order."

"But," he said with a condescending smile, "I can't be in two places at once. Mortalwood asked me to bring him a dry martini. A bourbon straight up for Fisk. And a ginger ale for your august self."

Whitney put a well-manicured hand on her hip. "Listen," she said in a tone she hadn't been forced to use in years, "go see he doesn't plow this boat into a reef or a porpoise or a shrimp boat or something."

"There aren't any shrimp boats," he corrected her smugly. "The shrimpers went on strike at midnight last night. Over shrimp prices. Or don't you pay attention to such lowly matters?"

"Listen," Whitney repeated, the danger rising in her tone. "Just get out there and keep an eye on him."

He laughed, showing a flash of even, white teeth. "I told you, miss. Right now, my orders are to fetch and carry."

"*I'll* make drinks," Whitney retorted. "You get out there and see that this boat doesn't lurch around anymore."

"You're sure?" He raised one eyebrow as if he were half bored, half dubious.

"I'm positive!" she said sharply. "*Out* there. You're supposed to be a captain—go and captain."

He shrugged and took a step toward the door. "Fine. Only make sure his majesty's martini is dry. With an onion, no olive. Pierce the onion halfway through. Understand?"

He ducked slightly to clear the low doorway, then looked back at her, smiling his superior smile. "And don't bruise the gin," he said.

Something in Whitney snapped. The most important deal in the company's history might be in the immediate offing, and she should be on deck, talking it over with Fisk and Mr. M. She should not be trapped here trying to cope with this maddeningly self-satisfied son of a sea cook.

Although she seldom allowed herself to show anger, she did so now. "I will see," she said between her teeth, "that you never work for Mr. Mortalwood again. I will also see that whoever recommended you for this job never recommends you for another. And—" she pointed her finger, leveling it at him like a gun "—if you don't act more civilly, I'll see you're put off this boat at Hilton Head and that somebody else is hired."

"Fine," he said, smiling so the dimples deepened. "I'm a free agent. I don't care. You people aren't up-front, anyway. What are you going to Sand Dollar for? I heard Mortalwood say he wanted to head for Sand Dollar. What's he doing? Not just testing this tub. He should have an engineer do that. I don't think this is a pleasure trip. I don't think people like you know how to have pleasure."

"Where we're going isn't any of your business," Whitney replied hotly. "Go do what *is* your business. And leave *me* alone."

"With pleasure. But first I should tell you something."

Whitney stared at him with hostility. He stood in the sunshine on the deck now, the wind tossing his dark blond hair.

"Before you waltz off to serve the high-muck-a-mucks," he said, "fix your lipstick. It's smeared."

Automatically she put her fingertips to her lips, as if she could feel the proof of what he said.

He grinned and drew his shirt back slightly from his chest. There, right across the blue alligator tattooed over his heart, was her scarlet lip print. She was horrified. It looked for all the world as if she'd kissed his bare chest.

"Wipe that off right now," Whitney ordered, her heart pummeling.

He shook his head. "I'll wear it proudly," he said, his grin more flippant than before. "Maybe I'll go around showing it off in bars. Well, don't stay in the kitchen all day. Though a woman's work is never done, I guess."

He sauntered off, hands in the pockets of his white shorts.

Angrily Whitney turned from the door and set about making fresh drinks. She was so irritated that her hands shook as she scrubbed the tray clean.

How dared he be so rude? For years people—both women and men—had treated her with respect, at first for her intelligence and hard work, and now for her position and power, as well.

She had foolishly allowed herself to be upset by a man who was no more than hired help. He was a nothing, a cipher, a nobody, she told herself furiously.

As far as she knew, he didn't even have a steady job. He must have taunted her because he was jealous. She was somebody, he wasn't, and his stupid male ego couldn't bear it. He wanted to think himself superior.

She took a deep breath to calm herself. He was nothing, she told herself again, a nonentity. But she was *someone;* she and her mother and Lila and Mr. M., too, had made her into someone. She was successful and independent and influential. Indeed, she, Lawrence Mortalwood and Adrian Fisk were the three most powerful people in an extremely powerful corporation.

And *if* Sand Dollar Island looked as good as it sounded, and *if* the corporation successfully snatched it off the market before anyone else knew it was on, then Whitney would be the most powerful woman in what had become a major corporation.

Empire, she thought with excitement. Empire was what the yacht sailed toward: a potential Mortalwood Kingdom. Which one day, with Mr. M.'s blessing, might be ruled by her capable hand alone.

So how, Whitney wondered, could one unshaven man, no better than a deckhand, addle her into momentarily forgetting about success and power and building empires?

Why did he make her feel like skinny little Whitney Shane of Kanker County again? He made her remember being an awkward teenager, passing the paper mill after school, head down, so she wouldn't have to see the young men lounging outside, taking their cigarette break.

They always seemed to have sex in their eyes, those men. She had been taught to fear, despise and avoid them, but she was safe from them now, safe forever. She had escaped them and the harsh world they symbolized.

She had lifted herself above men like Gabe Cantrell forever.

Carefully picking up the tray, she went to join the real men aboard, the men of wealth, influence and authority. She was part of their charmed circle now, one of their kind. She herself was a creature of rank and privilege and power.

CHAPTER TWO

"I DON'T KNOW what happened, if I hit something or what," Mr. Mortalwood fretted, sitting in his deck chair. Gabe Cantrell had taken over the wheel, and the yacht's course was once again smooth.

"It's these glasses," Mortalwood complained. "I can't get used to them. And the boat doesn't feel right. She's sluggish."

"Don't worry," Whitney said, handing him his martini. "We'll have everything checked when we get to Hilton Head."

She gave Adrian Fisk his bourbon and settled into another deck chair to the right of Mr. Mortalwood, holding her glass of ginger ale. She never drank during business hours, and this was a business trip. In the South many businessmen disapproved of women drinking, even at lunch. There were a thousand subtleties to being a female executive, and Whitney knew them all.

"We have a fine day to see the island," Adrian Fisk said, sipping his bourbon. He gazed at a map in his hand and then at Cantrell in the wheelhouse, checking that the man was out of earshot.

Mr. M. held a similar map and handed another to Whitney.

"It's a small island," Fisk said, "about five miles across at its widest. But it has slightly over eight miles of usable beach. That's what's pure gold."

Whitney nodded, studying the map. Sand Dollar was one of the tidal barrier islands. These islands, strung like a series of shields along the Georgia coast, caught the onslaught of the ocean's tide, protecting the marshy coast from its force. The sea had pounded the islands for centuries, so the islands, not the Georgia coastline, were where the beaches had formed.

Some islands, like Tybee, St. Simon's and Carolina's Hilton Head, had been developed. Some, like Sapelo, were settled in part, but not commercialized. A few, like Cumberland, were protected wilderness areas.

Sand Dollar, named for its nearly round shape, was unique in that it was owned completely by one person, Freda Fredericks. The island had belonged to her family for generations.

"No one at all lives on it?" Whitney asked, shaking her head in disapproval. "What a waste."

"A waste, indeed," Adrian agreed. He was an immaculately neat man, slender, dark-haired and dark-eyed. Whitney had never been able to guess his age. He might have been a mature-looking thirty-five or a well-preserved fifty; it was impossible to tell.

"Freda Fredericks used to spend her summers there, when her grandparents owned it," Adrian said. "But the main house and outbuildings burned to the ground over forty years ago, and they were never rebuilt. Weather's ruined the rest, but a dock's been kept intact."

Mr. M. took a breath of the sea air and exhaled with satisfaction. "Lord, I've missed this."

Adrian Fisk smoothed his hair, as if he didn't like it being mussed by the wind. "Mrs. Fredericks lets selected groups use the island from time to time. For wilderness camping. The rest of the time the place just sits there. Scandalous."

The bright green of the coastal marshes had almost disappeared behind them. Far out in the waves Whitney saw a dolphin playing, arcing out of the sea and diving back. She had seen few dolphins in her life and knew little of the sea. She repressed an urge to cry out and point at the animal. It wouldn't be businesslike, and business was being discussed.

She frowned, trying to concentrate. "You said Mrs. Fredericks had considered giving the land to the public," she said. "For another protected wilderness area. But her son thinks he can convince her to sell it?"

Adrian nodded. "Sheldon Fredericks. Yes. He thinks so. Lord, I wonder if I should go below and put on some sunscreen and get my hat."

"You're too vain, Adrian." Mr. Mortalwood laughed indulgently. "A little sun wouldn't hurt any of us. Even Whitney."

Whitney smiled politely. She tanned easily, but spent only a moderate amount of time in the sun. A dark tan would imply she was too fond of leisure, was not a serious and competent person. She tapped her gold pen against the map.

"What I don't understand," she said, "is why Sheldon Fredericks came to *us* instead of putting the place on the open market." It was the part of the deal that made her uneasy.

"I told you," Adrian said brusquely. "He knows we run an efficient outfit. He likes our style and thinks we'll appeal to the old woman."

Whitney raised one eyebrow. She didn't care for the way Adrian referred to Mrs. Fredericks as "the old woman," and she was certain Adrian knew more than he was saying. She didn't trust him, because she knew he wouldn't hesitate to advance himself in any way he could. She had better stay on guard.

"Quite frankly," Mr. Mortalwood said, not looking at Whitney, "he's also interested in stock."

Whitney straightened in her chair, giving Mr. M. an intent stare. "Stock? But you and Lila owned all the stock. She never wanted for you to part with any. This is the first I've heard—"

Mortalwood raised a plump hand to silence her. "It's all in the talking stage, Whitney, and highly confidential. Nothing's settled, not in the least."

"Well, I should hope not," she said firmly. "Before any stock changes hands, I'd want a thorough study of any such proposal. *And* see it discussed openly with the accounting people. Secrecy is sometimes necessary, but—"

"Secrecy is of the *utmost* importance in this case," Adrian interrupted, putting on his sunglasses. "We *cannot* let people know we're interested in this property. First, it would breed competition. Second, there's going to be one hell of an outcry if we pull this off, from conservation groups. It's going to take some excellent public-relations work to handle it."

Mortalwood put his hand to his forehead. "I don't even want to think about the conservation groups. They'll want to skin us alive. They'll want a bloodbath."

"Sand Dollar's prime real estate," Adrian said stonily. He flexed his pale hands enviously. "Some damn fools may want to keep it a sanctuary for raccoons and ticks and rattlesnakes. But we've got the potential for a multimillion-dollar development here."

The boat was passing one of the other islands. A lighthouse rose whitely from a green hillock, and sunlight played on the dancing waves. It was distractingly beautiful, and Whitney had to tear her curious attention away from the view to hear what Mr. Mortalwood was saying.

"I envisioned condos going in." He nodded sagely. "Both oceanfront and inland. Also a full-scale resort. Not only utilize the beach, but put in swimming pools, tennis courts, golf course, stables, a marina."

"Not stables." Adrian frowned. "Horses need pastures. I can't see wasting land on pastures. As for the golf course, that'll mean draining a marsh, but we could do it. It would be expensive, but cost-effective."

Whitney crossed her legs at the ankles as a lady should and tried to ignore another dolphin gamboling in the distance. "Once we've seen this place..."

"We'll see as much of it as we can from the boat," Mr. Mortalwood said, inhaling the salt air again. "Then we'll do what we can on foot. There are still roads left. Overgrown, I'm told, but we can walk them. Then it's off to Hilton Head to get down to the first phase of decision-making and brainstorming."

Whitney shook her head, still disturbed. Mr. Mortalwood was being extremely secretive about every detail of this trip. No one in the office, even, knew what they were doing. Lila, she was sure, wouldn't have liked it.

Adrian and Mortalwood had left the night before, on Monday, taking a late flight to Savannah. They had told everyone they were going to a development seminar at a rural retreat in Nova Scotia and would be gone until the end of the week.

Whitney had shown up at the office this morning to put her desk in order, then left immediately on the pretext of attending a wedding. Then, supposedly, she was to fly to Missouri to spend several days viewing retirement communities in the Ozarks that might serve as models for new Mortalwood projects.

Nobody except Sheldon Fredericks knew they were traveling to Sand Dollar, and even he might not know that this was the week. Mr. Mortalwood had chosen the week rather than the weekend because it would be a less expected move, and in October, fewer pleasure boats would be about, and therefore fewer observers.

So secret did Mr. M. wish this early phase to remain that he refused even to go back to Atlanta after seeing Sand Dollar. Instead, they were to go to the most exclusive and secluded resort at Hilton Head where they would stay until Saturday. To ensure confidentiality, Mr. M. had personally registered them under assumed names.

A speck appeared in the distance in the east, a greenish dot amidst the gray waves. A pelican flew over the boat, its great wings gliding smoothly on the wind.

"There it is," Mr. M. said excitedly, gesturing at the speck. "That's it. The island. I think I'd like to take the boat in myself. Then we can look, moving at exactly the pace I want. By God, this is something, isn't it?"

He rose from his deck chair. Whitney looked up at him with a slight surge of alarm. "Mr. M., do you think you should? I mean, do you know these waters?"

He patted her shoulder. "Whitney, you're a landlubber. You told me so yourself. Don't worry. Besides, I want to check the steering again. Something about her just doesn't feel right. That captain couldn't notice. He doesn't know her, not the way I do."

He shuffled off toward the helm, looking happier than Whitney had seen him look in months.

"I'm going below to put on some sunscreen," Adrian Fisk said irritably. "And some insect repellent. I hate hiking through tall grass—there are *bugs*. There are rattlesnakes on that island, too. You should have brought something sturdier than those sandals."

He rose, nodding critically at her expensive sandals. He wore tall leather boots that made him look a bit like the stereotype of a dictatorial movie director.

Whitney smiled to herself. Adrian didn't know it, but a rattlesnake could bite through the leather of his boots as effortlessly as it bit through a steer's hide. She had learned that long ago, when she'd lived in her grandmother's house in the piny woods near the river's edge.

But Adrian wouldn't believe she knew anything about snakes, and even if he did, he would only grow more fretful about the prospect of meeting one.

She rose and went to the rail to stare out at the island. It grew larger as the boat approached, a green shadow, edged with white. The white, she thought, smiling, had to be the beach. The highly desirable and extremely valuable beach. The beach that could make the Mortalwood Corporation into the Mortalwood Kingdom.

"Why are you staring so hard? Thinking of buying it?"

Gabe Cantrell's voice startled her, but she tried to keep from showing it. She didn't turn to look at him. "It's about the only thing to look at out here," she said curtly. "Shouldn't you be with Mr. Mortalwood, making sure he doesn't run aground or something?"

"Yes," he agreed, mockery in his voice, "I should. The electrical system in this tub stinks. But he wants to play sailor, and he doesn't want me staring over his shoulder. He told me to bring you this."

He stepped to her side and handed her a small camera in a case. She understood. Although Mortalwood already had pictures of the property, he wanted her to take more, for comparison. Wordlessly she zipped open the case. It was a simple camera, easy to use, loaded and ready.

She could feel Cantrell's gaze on her, hear his shirt flapping in the wind. Out of the corner of her eye she could see his hard lean hands on the rail.

"What are you to the old guy, anyway?" he asked with casual impertinence. "Secretary? Personal assistant? Girlfriend?"

She snapped her head up to stare at him with dislike. "I'm an executive," she said. "I happen to be a vice president at his company."

"My," he said, pretending to be impressed. "An executive. A pretty young thing like you. A vice president. Wow."

His sun-streaked hair blew in the wind, and as usual, his eyes were narrowed against the glare of the sun. He still hadn't buttoned his shirt, but the tattooed alligator adorned by her lipstick mercifully didn't show.

He had a knowing smile that she'd seen on other men's faces, the sort of smile she didn't like. "If I ever have a company, I'm going to get me a pretty young vice president. For my very own." He smiled, insolence in the curve of his mouth.

"My age, appearance and sex have nothing to do with my having this job," she informed him icily.

"I didn't say they did," he tossed back. He leaned his elbows on the rail and watched the island as they approached.

"He's turning this thing," he observed. "Going to take us on a tour all the way around, isn't he? What's got him interested in this island, anyway? What kind of company are you vice president of?"

"Your job isn't to ask questions," Whitney said shortly. "And mine isn't to answer when you do."

"All right," he agreed with a laconic shrug, not bothering to look at her. "Just trying to make civil conversation. I'll work it out for myself, instead. Your, er, employer is obviously prosperous—although he doesn't know much about boats. The three of you aren't from around here. You came in from Atlanta, although not together."

Whitney glanced at his profile apprehensively. He had a fine aquiline nose, and his tan, his dark blond hair and his strong jawline made him look like a Viking chieftain, staring out thoughtfully over the waves, brooding about the strategy for an upcoming battle.

"How do you know that?" she demanded suspiciously. The man couldn't be some sort of corporate spy, could he? Once again she was uncomfortably aware that he was far more intelligent than she had anticipated.

He shrugged, watching the waves froth at the island's shoreline. "The men got here first. They had time to dress for the boat. You didn't. You still had the airline tag on your luggage. The three of you have the look of people who work together—a closed club. What's Fisk do? He defers to Mortalwood, and he pretends to defer to you, but he doesn't like you much. I'd watch your back if I were you."

"Mr. Fisk and I are colleagues and we get along just fine, thank you," Whitney retorted, her chin in the air.

He gave her a brief sideways glance. Both malice and humor glinted in his gray eyes. "You mean you think you have the upper hand. You may have—for now. That's why he looks at you the way he does. Right now you're golden, but he wants to be. Whatever you three are up to, he's more tense about it than you are. And you're all tense. Very tense. Something big is up, right?"

Whitney took a deep breath, stayed silent, trying to force herself to ignore him. *He's too smart,* she thought. *Way too smart. I'll tell Mr. Mortalwood. We'll pay him off to keep quiet. He probably needs money.*

She gazed out at the island. She could now clearly see the stretch of gray-white beach. Beyond it lay the bright green of marsh grasses, and beyond that the darker, shadowy green of forest, pine and live oak.

Mortalwood was bringing the yacht closer to shore on the far side of the island, its eastern side. Other than a few cruising sea gulls, there was no sign of life on the island, and except for their yacht, the sea seemed completely empty.

Whitney put the camera to her eye and pressed the automatic zoom button to bring the scene closer. It was a nice stretch of beach, she thought, but not wide. Still, it had possibilities. She bit her lower lip in concentration.

Gabe spoke again, his tone sardonic. "Why do I get the feeling you're closing in on this place like an enemy agent?"

"Look," she said impatiently, lowering the camera, "if you want to play detective, open an agency. And if you want to make yourself useful, get me another ginger ale. With three ice cubes. Not two, not four. Three. And make sure everything's packed for our picnic lunch when we land. Mr. Mortalwood's going to be hungry."

Smiling unpleasantly, Gabe stepped back from the rail and executed a small, neat bow, with all the flourish of a courtier. "I leap to do your bidding."

It was a surprisingly quick and graceful movement, yet his wind-tossed appearance made it seem profoundly out of place. She was aware that once again he had insulted her, and she vowed there would be no more of it.

We'll get rid of him at Hilton Head, she thought bitterly. *He's dangerous, and he's insolent, too.*

The next thing she knew a low, terrible sound thundered, shaking the air and half deafening her. Water spouted into the sky, raining down on her, and debris flew, falling and spinning around her.

She was caught in Gabe Cantrell's arms; he was all that had kept her from being flung to the deck. Something hard struck her in the back, something else struck her shoulder and bounced off. She buried her face against his chest, protecting her eyes from the rain of wreckage.

The deck made such a huge, odd and sickening movement that she opened her eyes, looking around wildly. The bow of the boat seemed to rise magically out of the water, as if trying to point at the noon sun, and the deck was sliding from beneath her feet. A rumbling sound filled the air.

Gabe pressed himself against the rail for balance, still holding her to his chest, his legs braced to fight the deck's sudden and insane tilt.

What...? Whitney thought, but she was too confused to speak. The boat's stern had tipped perilously close to the ocean, and she was amazed and terrified to see ocean water foaming up onto the deck.

A smell of smoke stung the air, and scraps of rubble floated on the water that churned behind them. "Hang on to the rail," Gabe yelled in her ear. "Stay high as you can." He pushed her against the railing, his hands closing powerfully over hers to make sure she gripped it tightly. Then he lurched away, the black-and-white shirt flying wildly behind him.

We're sinking, Whitney thought, sick with horror. *We hit something. Or something exploded. Or...*

All of her powers of reasoning stopped, paralyzed, as she heard Adrian Fisk screaming with terror from the cabin below. She looked about desperately for Mr. M. but couldn't see him; she could see nobody at all in the wheelhouse. Had he been thrown to the deck, injured?

Terrified, she called for him, but there was no answer. She clung to the rail so hard that her hands ached, but she had difficulty staying upright. She found herself sliding down toward the litter-filled water that swept over the stern.

Gabe Cantrell was making his way around the tilting deck like an acrobat, somehow keeping his balance. He pulled a lifeboat from its fastenings, grabbed a box marked First Aid, then half-lunged, half-crawled back to her, his teeth set in determination.

The yacht couldn't be sinking, Whitney told herself in disbelief, not this fast, it was unbelievable; how could something like this happen so swiftly?

Water splashed over the stern now, frothing higher on the deck each moment. She again heard Adrian Fisk's scream from below the deck. What if he was trapped? she thought in horror. She could still smell smoke. What if the boat was burning, as well as sinking, and Adrian was caught?

And where was Mr. M.? She cried out for him again, but heard nothing except the slap and sizzle and swallow of the waves. Her ears still rang painfully, disorienting her. Something must have exploded, she thought in confusion. But where? It had to be somewhere under the waterline—the engine itself?

"Come on," Gabe said roughly, trying to wrestle her, the lifeboat and the box safely down the stern. "Move! Grab your purse, grab anything you can, and *move*."

"I can't," she protested, fighting to stay where she was. By instinct, however, she snatched at her purse before it slid away, throwing the strap over her shoulder. "Don't worry about me. Find Mr. Mortalwood. And Fisk—Fisk needs help."

"Look," he said, and the expression on his face was savage, "I can only handle one of you at a time. Don't make trouble. Come *here*."

He hurled the inflated lifeboat out into the water with a muscle-wrenching heave. Water plumed up around it as it landed right side up. Then, still holding the first-aid box, he jerked Whitney to him by her arm, and half-dragged, half-carried her down the tilting deck.

The lifeboat bumped on the waves only a few yards from the sinking stern. "Get in. You're going to get wet, but get *in*," he ordered. He pushed her toward the boat.

Water surged up over her sandals, soaking the bottoms of her slacks. "I have to find Mr. M.," she screamed, trying to fight her way back up the deck.

"I'll find him," Gabe snarled. Somehow, she was in his arms, and then they were both in the gray, swelling sea. He kicked his way to one side of the lifeboat and pitched the first-aid box into it. He forced her to clamp her hands around the guide rope as he maneuvered the boat farther from the yacht.

"Get in," he ordered again. "I'll hold it steady."

But Whitney saw something white floating off among the debris off the sinking stern—Mr. M.'s new yachting cap. Then she saw Mr. M. himself, his face dazed and disbelieving, rising out of the water. He had lost his glasses and was choking and gasping.

"I can get him," Whitney shouted at Gabe. "I can handle him. Get Fisk and get on the radio. Get help."

Gabe looked at her in angry disbelief, but she had already flung her purse into the raft and was efficiently stroking her way through the water. She moved faster than Gabe moved even, reaching Mr. M. just as he sank beneath the surface again. She held her breath, dove and slung her arm around Mr. M.'s neck, working herself into a position to get him into a lifesaving hold. Expertly she pulled him to the surface and towed him, limp, toward the raft.

Gabe watched her, the set of his mouth still fierce, but he apparently decided she knew what she was doing. He turned back toward the sinking yacht with powerful, determined strokes.

Salt stung Whitney's eyes, and her ears vibrated insanely from the crash or the explosion, but she could still hear Fisk screaming.

She would have to leave him to Gabe Cantrell to save, she thought fatalistically. If she let go of Mr. M. he would drown.

"Hang on," she gasped to Mortalwood. "I've got you."

He didn't try to resist; he seemed too disoriented, almost helpless, passive as a badly frightened child.

She tried with all her strength to hoist him up into the safety of the little boat, but she could not.

With one hand she clung to the side of the raft, with her other arm she kept Mr. M.'s face out of the water. He had a scrape and a bruise on his forehead. "Lila?" he asked, still choking from the water he'd swallowed. "Lila? Lila?"

"Everything's fine, everything's fine," Whitney said, hoping he didn't hear the desperation in her voice. She glanced at the shore, measuring its distance. She could swim that far and handle Mr. M. She was sure of that.

Little girl what lives by the side of the river had better know how to swim, sure as shootin', her uncle Dub had often said after she had moved in with her grandmother. And he had taught her. *That child swims like a 'gator,* he'd tell people. *Yessirree.*

She gritted her teeth. She'd swim like a 'gator, all right, supporting Mr. M. and pulling the raft if she had to.

The yacht, she saw with horror, was already more than half underwater, its bow pulpit pointing skyward. She could no longer see Gabe or hear Adrian Fisk's cries for help.

Her heart froze to deadness as she watched the boat sinking swiftly beneath the waves. What if Gabe Cantrell and Fisk were both trapped inside, unable to escape? A thick cloud of smoke hung in the air. What if fire threatened them, as well as water?

She didn't dare release Mr. M. and try to make her way to the yacht and see if she could help.

"Lila," Mr. M. almost wept, his voice broken, "are we all right?"

"We're fine," Whitney whispered, trying to hold him more securely as she clung to the side of the lifeboat.

The waves slapped and hissed. Gigantic bubbles gulped out of the water as the boat sank deeper. The wind sighed over the waves.

Then, with frightening speed and a long, final gurgle, the last of the boat sank. More bubbles rushed to the surface. Then there was silence, unbroken except for the low moan of the sea and the sharp cry of the gulls.

They're dead, Whitney thought in despair. Fisk and Cantrell were both dead, and she was alone in the sea with Mr. M., and he was hurt, who knew how badly? What could she do with him, alone on the island, once she got him there?

Suddenly with a great roil of water, Gabe Cantrell's head broke the surface of the waves. He sputtered, shaking water from his eyes. He gasped for breath so raggedly the sound seemed ripped out of his chest.

"Cantrell!" Whitney cried joyously. His dark blond hair, plastered to his skull, looked almost black with wetness, and his face was contorted with the hunger for air. To Whitney, however, at that glorious moment, he looked beautiful.

He raised his arm as high as he could. He was holding an unconscious Adrian Fisk by his shirt collar. Adrian's skin was grayish blue and he had a split lip and bruised jaw.

Gabe struggled to get the man in an awkward lifesaving carry, then bore him toward the raft. "You all right?" he asked in a raw voice, throwing Whitney a cursory glance.

"Fine, but I can't get him in the boat," she panted, still holding Mr. M. He had lapsed into silence again, his eyes half-closed, fluttering spasmodically.

Grimacing with effort, Gabe flung Adrian Fisk's body up so that the man lay in a crumpled, limp bundle on the bottom of the raft.

"Is he all right?" Whitney asked, frightened again. Adrian looked half-dead.

"He'll live," Gabe said shortly, still fighting for oxygen to feed his famished lungs. "Here. Give me Mortalwood. Hold the boat steady. I'll get him in, too."

Together she and Gabe struggled to raise Mr. M.'s heavy body and roll him into the boat. At last Whitney was forced to clamber into the raft herself and pull on the older man as Gabe, still fighting for breath, pushed from beneath.

At last Mortalwood sagged into the boat, his body falling against Adrian's, causing Adrian to moan. Adrian looked in far worse shape than Mr. M. did, Whitney thought, frightened, so she rolled him onto his stomach as best she could and started trying to press the water out of his lungs. It was awkward in the little boat, but at last he groaned again and stirred.

Her pulses leapt in relief. Both men in the raft were alive, and it seemed possible to pull them back into consciousness.

She pressed as hard as she could on Adrian's back, forcing his lungs to work harder. He spit water, choked, and at last he swore at her. "Leave me alone," he managed to demand in a feeble, querulous voice.

She looked out at Gabe Cantrell, who was now towing the boat, swimming steadily toward shore, his breath a thick, painful panting. "Get in," she ordered. "It's crowded, but there's room for you."

"We lost the paddle," he managed to say. "This is the only way we'll get to shore."

Inwardly Whitney swore. Adrian lay, shivering and whimpering, on the raft's bottom. Beside him, curled in an almost fetal position, lay Mr. M. His eyes, although half-opened, seemed unseeing, but his breathing was regular, if somewhat shallow.

Gabe Cantrell struggled to tow the three of them against the tide to the shore. He was making progress, but she could see how tautly his arm muscles stretched and worked as he pulled the raft, and hear how laboriously he breathed.

"I'll help," she muttered without enthusiasm. She slipped out of the boat and back into the water. For the first time she noticed how cold the sea was.

"What the hell?" Gabe asked, looking at her in disbelief.

She grabbed another of the raft's safety lines and began to tow, able to keep pace with him, although she didn't know for how long. She thought she heard another explosion, but she wasn't sure, because her heart was beating so loudly in her ringing ears.

At a surprisingly fair distance from shore, the water grew shallow enough to stand. First Gabe could touch down, then she could. Together they tugged and pulled the awkward little raft, the surf crashing around their bodies. Whitney quickly learned to time when the waves struck so that she could leap against their pull, dodge their power and precariously keep her balance.

At last, staggering with effort as they pulled the boat, they reached the shore, Gabe a pace or two ahead of her. Water streamed from his lean body. Whitney stumbled after him, as soaked and sodden as he. When he gave the final tug that pulled the lifeboat past the water's edge, she added another tug of her own, determined to pull it an inch farther, an inch nearer to safety.

She and Gabe barely looked at one another. They worked in unspoken unison, their breathing arduous. He half-dragged, half-carried Mortalwood to the shelter of a sand dune where a stand of sea wheat waved, casting its thin shadow. Gabe rolled the man over, applied pressure to his back to expel whatever Mr. M. had wrongly swallowed or breathed.

Whitney, surprised at her own strength, pulled Adrian Fisk to his feet. He was conscious but groggy, and he sank against her. She let him lean all his weight on her and led him, limping badly, to the dune to sit down beside Mr. Mortalwood.

Adrian coughed and swore, then fell on his side. "Don't touch me," he warned Whitney. "Just let me lie here. Get me a blanket. Get me some dry clothes. Get me water."

Then his face crumpled slightly, and he wept against the sand. "Leave me alone," he ordered again. "Just leave me alone, dammit!"

Mortalwood, beside him, opened his eyes completely and breathed deeply. Then he astonished Whitney by beginning to smile. His troubled face went smoothly childlike, and he began to talk to Lila. Then he went silent again and simply stared happily into space.

Whitney turned to go back to the raft for the first-aid kit. Exhausted, she stumbled and fell to her hands and knees, then she fought her way to her feet again.

"Stop," Gabe muttered, putting his hand on her arm, keeping her from trying to stagger back to the raft. "He's in slight shock, that's all. I'll raise his feet. Sit. Rest."

Whitney stood numbly, but was unable to move. She stared down as Gabe stripped off his shirt and put it under Mr. M.'s head, fashioning a crude pillow. A heap of gleaming seaweed draped the foot of the dune. Gabe gathered it into a ragged heap and pushed it under Mr. M.'s ankles and knees, elevating his legs.

Wearily he stood and looked down at her. "Sit," he repeated. "Rest. Then we'll do what we can for them."

He forced her to move to a neighboring dune, less sheltered than the one where the two men lay. The sun blissfully warmed Whitney's sea-chilled skin. The hot sand beneath her feet felt comforting and wonderfully solid, but her knees shook from stress and exertion.

"Sit down," he said, lowering himself to the sand tiredly, keeping hold of her arm. Gratefully, she let herself sink beside him, almost prayerfully happy at the firmness of the earth beneath her.

She wanted to ask him what had happened to the yacht, what had happened to Fisk, how Gabe had saved him and where help was to come from. She hadn't the strength to ask any of these questions. She clasped her arms around her bent knees and pressed her face against her arms. She shuddered.

He put his arm around her, drawing her up and near to him so that she could lean back, exhausted, against his chest. He was like the earth itself, she thought numbly. Strong, solid, dependable, *safe*.

"You're all right?" he asked.

She nodded, still too wrung out by exertion to speak.

"You're sure?"

She nodded again.

He stroked her wet hair and she raised her eyes to his.

His bronze lashes were starred with water, the expression on his face showed his familiar intentness mixed with fatigue, but something new glittered in his eyes. He was looking at her differently than he had on the boat.

"What about you?" she asked huskily, her voice weak. "Are you all right?"

He managed approximately a quarter inch of a smile. "A little beat up. You helped a lot. You're a good swimmer."

Her heart skipped a beat for unwarranted reasons. "I swim like a 'gator," she breathed. She didn't know why she said that. She realized that when she did, her old accent came back, her piny-woods country accent, just for a moment. She didn't care.

She bit her lip, trying to force strength back into her body. But no strength came, and her lip tasted salty.

His gray eyes stayed trained on her blue ones, as if he was trying to read some story deep within them.

"What happened to the yacht?" she asked, looking away from him. Her hair had come loose and she felt the wind blowing it about her shoulders.

He drew her close to him to rest against his chest again. She did not have the energy to protest. It felt too wonderful to feel somebody else's warmth, somebody else's vitality, another person's nearness after the terror of the water.

"I don't know," he said simply. "I think there was an explosion."

"What happens next?" she asked, leaning against his shoulder and closing her eyes. She could hear Adrian Fisk, softly weeping, barely audible over the sound of the wind and the waves.

"I don't know that, either," he said. His stubbled jaw was prickly against her ear. "But nobody's hurt too badly. We'll make it."

Nobody's hurt too badly, she thought, faint with gratitude at the words. *We'll make it.* Fresh courage surged through her, and she leaned more comfortably against Gabe, from whom the courage came.

She squeezed her eyes shut more tightly. They still stung from seawater. It did not seem odd or wrong to lean against Gabe or let his arm encircle her, keeping her close to the warmth of his body.

She felt a strange bond of camaraderie with him that she was too exhausted to question. Perhaps it was a silent communion they shared at having survived, and having helped the others to survive.

"Who's going to help us?" she asked, trusting him to have the answer.

He said nothing for a long moment. He stroked her hair again. Once more she could hear Adrian's muffled sobs. She turned her face away, hoping the wind would no longer carry the sound to her ears.

Gabe Cantrell shifted her so that she almost lay in the crook of his arm. "Look at me," he ordered.

She opened her eyes, blinking up at him in surprise.

He stared down at her solemnly. "*Nobody's* going to help us. We have to help ourselves. Understand? Are you up to it?"

She blinked again. The breeze tossed his damp, gold hair about his face, a tangled, dancing mane.

"We have to help ourselves," he repeated.

She stared up at him fearfully, the import of his words sinking in. There had been no time to radio for help. No other ship had been nearby to see their boat go down. They were alone on the most isolated of the islands for who knew how long. Her heart stumbled at the thought.

"It's all right," he said, brushing back a strand of her hair. "We'll make it."

His face hovered above hers, his eyes locked on hers. She was not surprised when he bent his face closer to hers, but she was frightened. All the old fears came rushing back to her, but she was too tired to fully register the crowd and push of them.

She closed her eyes as he bent nearer still and kissed her. His lips, too, tasted of salt. He touched her cheek, and she could feel the sand clinging to his fingertips. The sun beat down on both their damp bodies, and her wet sweater flapped in the wind, rustling against his bare chest.

It was all right to kiss him, she thought dreamily. It was a natural gesture, a celebration of survival. His mouth burned against hers and her senses danced dizzily, giddy with joy that she was still alive and still could feel, still could touch. He laced his fingers through her blowing hair and kissed her more deeply, his tongue tracing first the curve of her lips, then the secrets within.

The fears that weariness had held at bay swarmed back, a pack of goblins.

"Don't," she protested, trying to push away.

"Shh," he said, and pulled her back in his arms. He sank back into the sand, just holding her. "Just rest," he murmured, burying his face against her blowing hair. "Just rest a minute."

And Whitney, suddenly wanting rest more than she wanted anything on earth, didn't fight him. She lay in his arms, feeling as if she was slowly coming back to life. Perhaps Gabe felt the same way, and that was why he held her so fast.

CHAPTER THREE

"WHITNEY, I'M COLD. I want water. And my medicine."
Mr. M.'s voice sounded weak.

Dazed, Whitney opened her eyes, trying to raise on her elbow. Gabe pulled her back. "His medicine? What medicine?" he demanded, holding her against him and staring into her eyes.

"Whitney? Whitney?" called Mr. M. like a groggy, frightened child.

Gabe's heart drummed against her breast, and her own heart dipped crazily. His eyes had their familiar intensity, almost a fierceness. "What medicine?"

Whitney pushed away from him with a fierceness of her own. She sat, her head aching. Too many cares and fears came rushing over her.

"His medicine," she said unhappily, pushing her damp hair back, "his blood-pressure medicine, his ulcer medicine, his allergy medicines, his tranquillizers, his sleeping pills."

Gabe sat up, gritting his teeth. "The man's a basket case."

Whitney rose shakily to her feet and made her way to Mr. M. He struggled to sit but fell back with a weak groan. She sank beside him on her knees, taking his hand. His skin was cold, but awareness shone from his eyes at last.

On Mortalwood's other side, Adrian Fisk lay, curled in a knot. Whitney couldn't see his face and the sound of his weeping had stopped, but his fists were clenched as if in anguish or impotent anger.

"Mr. M.," Whitney said, "let me look in your pockets." He still wore his navy blazer, but it was ripped and sand clung to its wet folds.

"Water, Whitney," he said, looking up into her face. He recognized her, and that was good, she told herself. She patted his hand.

"I'm cold. It hurts to sit up. It hurts *here*." Mortalwood put a trembling hand over his ribs and winced.

Frantically Whitney searched his pockets. He cried out when she gently tried to turn him to reach into his side pocket. *Oh, no, he's got a broken rib,* she thought sickly. *What if he punctured a lung?*

"You'll be all right, Mr. M.," she tried to assure him. "Look. I've found your aspirins. That'll help. Here. Take two."

She put her arm beneath his head so he could raise himself. "I need water," he grimaced.

"We haven't got any," she told him. "Just take them." She used the same stern, no-nonsense tone she often used on her younger cousins when she'd had to tend them years ago. Miraculously it worked. He took the two aspirins into his mouth, then lay back, his lips twisting at the bitterness of the pills.

She was relieved to hear Gabe ask, "What's the story?" She sensed him standing behind her even before his shadow fell over her.

She glanced up, showing him the tin of pills. "I found some aspirin. They're damp, and maybe there're eight or nine left. I think he has a broken rib."

Gabe carried the white first-aid box with its red cross. He knelt beside her, opened it, then swore. "This stuff is ancient," he grumbled, inspecting the contents. "Why didn't anybody keep up things?"

"We'll have to do with what we've got," Whitney said firmly. "What's wrong with Adrian? I can tell his foot's hurt. And he was knocked out. By the explosion? You tend to him. I'll take care of Mr. M."

Gabe gave her a slow smile that wasn't pleasant. "Orders already? No. The explosion didn't knock Fisk out. I did. You'd better tend him. I don't think he's happy with me."

Whitney, who had loosened Mr. Mortalwood's collar and was feeling his brow, stopped in midmotion. Her hand rested on the older man's forehead. "You *hit* Adrian?" she asked, horrified.

"He was trapped and panicked," Gabe almost snarled. "His leg was pinned under a bunk. The water was rising. I had to sprain his ankle—maybe break it—to get him free. By that time, he was fighting me, and the only way to get us both out of there was to stun him. So I did."

She looked at him in dismay, remembering Adrian's split lip and bruised jaw. Adrian was proud; he would never forgive such an affront, never.

Gabe Cantrell, a bitter smile still crooking his mouth, suddenly reminded her of a blond savage as he squatted beside Mr. M. The sunlight bounced off his naked, golden shoulders.

"Go see if Fisk has stopped crying," he said. "I'll check Mortalwood. I've probably got more experience with this kind of thing."

She stared at him a long moment. He returned her gaze stonily, then turned to Mr. M. "Where's it hurt, buddy?' he asked the older man. "Here? Here? Let's take a look." Expertly, effortlessly, he maneuvered Mr. M. into a sitting position without making him wince or cry out.

Whitney set her jaw. So Cantrell was taking charge, was he? That was fine—for the time being. She'd tend to him later. For now she turned her attention from him and rummaged through the first-aid kit, then made her way to Adrian. She knelt beside him.

His fists were still clenched and his eyes squeezed shut.

"Adrian," she said softly, "are you all right? Is your ankle throbbing? Are you hurt anywhere else?"

Adrian curled into a tighter knot, as if he could burrow into the sand and disappear from his pain.

"I'm going to clean your face," Whitney told him. "Then we'll look at your ankle. Can you sit?"

"Go away," Adrian ordered petulantly. "Go do something useful. Find me water. I can take care of myself."

"Adrian, I have to know how you are," she said, trying to reason with him. "Here. Roll over."

He fought her weakly as she tried to roll him onto his back so she could treat his face. But at last he stopped struggling and simply lay there, his face rigid with torment. She took a gauze pad, wet it with alcohol, and wiped the sand from his face. The bruise was an ugly one and the cut on his lip deep.

No wonder Adrian was peevish and full of childish rancor, she thought, swabbing the cut. He must have lost control of himself, something she had never imagined him doing. Gabe must have knocked him nearly to kingdom come.

Adrian flinched and cursed when she put iodine on his cut, and she almost flinched herself, but repressed the urge. Squeamishness would only make her less effective.

"I know it burns," she said, her voice tightening, "but it has to be done. Lie still or you'll get sand in that cut. I'll look at your ankle. Do you want to sit?"

"Do something *useful*," Adrian complained, his eyes screwing shut more tightly. "Get help. Leave me alone. Get help—that's an order."

"We'll talk about orders later," she told him, tempered steel in her tone. "I can't do anything until I know how badly you're hurt."

She glanced at Gabe, who bent over Mortalwood, expertly wrapping a bandage around the older man's pale chest. He was obviously handling his patient with greater success than she was hers.

Gabe glanced over at Whitney, one brow drawn down. She looked away, embarrassed. She didn't like his seeing the trouble she had handling Adrian. She also felt oddly shamed to see so much of Mr. M.'s pale, flaccid flesh. Next to him, Gabe looked all the more like a man from a harsher, more primitive world, work-hardened and sun-burnished. Almost furtively, she looked at the two of them again.

"He's only bruised," Gabe told her brusquely, nodding at Mortalwood. "And he's pulled some muscles. How's my friend over there? Can you get that fool boot off him?"

Suddenly Adrian rose on his elbow, his eyes snapping open. They flashed darkly as he looked at Gabe with resentment. "You broke my ankle," he accused. "You *assaulted* me. When we get back, you'll hear from my attorneys, I promise you. You'll pay for this, believe me."

Adrian's voice shook with anger and his glare should have been riveting, but Gabe didn't seem bothered. "Take your boot off, Fisk," he ordered curtly. "If you can't pull it off, have the lady cut it off." He reached into the pocket of his white shorts and produced a red pocketknife, which he tossed carelessly to Whitney.

"There, Mortalwood," Gabe said, turning back to Mr. M., his tone kinder. "Get your shirt back on so you don't get sunburned. Then lie down. Keep those feet up. You're still in shock."

Mr. M. struggled feebly back into his shirt, then lay down with a grateful sigh. Gabe covered him with the damp blazer as best he could.

Then Gabe stood, looking down at the three of them. He towered over them, giving Whitney an unpleasant sensation. "I've got some questions—" he began.

"Whitney," Mr. M. said, his voice quivering, "please bring me water."

"I'll try," Whitney answered, although she had no idea where water was to be found. "Just let me help Adrian with his ankle."

She reached for Adrian's booted foot, but he twitched away from her irritably. "I'll do it *myself*." He sat up straighter and began tugging ineffectually at the boot, his face contorting in pain. The boot wouldn't budge.

"Your ankle must be swollen," Whitney said. "Let's cut the boot—"

"Give me that!" Adrian ordered, snatching the knife from her.

"I said," Gabe repeated, a dangerous edge to his voice, "I have some questions."

"Go to hell," Adrian retorted and began sawing at the expensive leather of his boot. "You've probably crippled me, you goon, you lout—"

"Come here," Gabe commanded, reaching for Whitney and pulling her to her feet. He made no attempt to be polite. "I'm talking to *you*."

No wonder Adrian hated this man, she thought darkly. She resented Gabe's harsh grip on her wrist, the way he pulled her, protesting, out of hearing range of the others.

The tumble of the waves and the rush of the wind filled her ears, and his touch inflamed her with indignation. "Let go," she snapped, pulling her arm free. "Don't get physical with me. I don't like it, and I won't stand for it."

He ignored her anger, obviously angry himself. He put his hands on his lean hips and stared down at her. "I said I've got questions," he said, his lips curling. "Mortalwood's still fuzzy and Fisk is meaner than a cut snake. I want answers, I want them fast, and I want them straight. First, how soon are you three going to be missed?"

She blinked up at him, her anger suddenly fading. The seriousness of what he was asking sank into her consciousness.

"Nobody knew you were coming to Sand Dollar, did they?" he asked, his tone accusing.

She shook her head slowly, wishing she didn't have to admit it. "No. Nobody knew."

"You were going on to Hilton Head. How long before they miss you there?"

The sun seemed to beat down too hard, oppressing her, making her head ache. Gabe's hair glittered as it stirred in the breeze, and its brightness hurt her eyes. She licked her lips, which were dry.

When she didn't answer, he shifted his weight impatiently. He had lost his shoes in the wreck, and the white shorts were all he wore. They fluttered against his sinewy thighs.

"Look." His brows drew together in a frown. "You seem to have trouble getting this. Here it is in plain terms. We sent no radio message that we were in trouble. Nobody saw us go down. Now all anybody can see of that yacht is a little wreckage and an oil slick the tide is taking out. Soon not much of either will be left. It'll be as if that boat never existed. Understand?"

She understood but said nothing. She knew that what she must tell him was too terrible to utter, but she had to say it. All the muscles in her face felt paralyzed, dead.

He sighed harshly and bent closer so that she had to look into his eyes. "It's an easy question, Miss Shane. How soon before they miss you on Hilton Head? Before they start looking for you?"

Whitney's mouth went drier than before. Once more she had the giddy sensation of being dazzled by the sun and how it glinted off the man standing before her. The wind rattled in her ears and the sea rumbled. She opened her mouth, but it took a moment for her to form the words.

"They won't miss us," she said thickly. "We were registered under other names. All they'll know...is that a certain party hasn't shown up. They'll just think we changed our minds."

He made a sound of exasperation and glanced briefly heavenward, as if hoping for a miracle. Then he put his hands on her shoulders and forced her to meet his eyes again.

His touch jarred through her nerve ends like an electrical shock. "I told you," she said, indignant again but nervous, too, "don't get physical."

His hands tightened on her shoulders. "I'm trying to get *mental* with you, lady. What about back in Atlanta? Are you supposed to check in with people there? Who'll miss you?"

His face had grown increasingly tense. Whitney licked her dry lips again and felt slightly dazed by the beating sun. She shook her head. They had been too clever for their own good. "Nobody'll miss us. Not until the weekend at least. We all had cover stories. Nobody knows we're here."

He gripped her shoulders hard enough to hurt her, and when she tried to flinch away, he didn't let her.

"The weekend?" he said tonelessly. "It's only Tuesday. You mean nobody might catch on that you're missing until Saturday or Sunday? My God, why the secrecy? What are you up to?"

"What we're up to is beside the point," Whitney said desperately. "How soon will somebody find us?"

A cold smile twisted his mouth. "Good question. I've got nobody, and nobody'll be looking for me, that's for sure. Usually the only boats in these waters are the shrimpers. And they're on strike. A pleasure boat? Maybe. But probably not. We're off the beaten path."

Whitney stared at him, trying to keep all emotion from her face. When they had reached the shore, she had thought they were safe, or nearly so. Now she realized the danger could truly just be beginning. "You're saying..." she breathed, but couldn't finish.

"I'm saying we might be discovered this afternoon—or we might be here for days. *Days.* Understand me?"

She nodded numbly.

"So we have to *think*. How bad is Mortalwood's health? How crucial is his medicine? Should I go back out into the water now and dive—try to find his medication? *Could* I find it?"

She nodded again, confused. "His pills would be in his briefcase. I don't know if you could find it. Maybe he'll be all right—as long as nothing worse happens to him. He's got a number of health problems. The blood pressure is the worst."

He took a deep breath, clenched her shoulders more tightly. "All right. Then I'll wait and hope. So the first thing is to find water. Then shelter and food."

She looked about them helplessly. The endless stretches of ocean, gray and saturated with salt, swayed as if to mock them. She stared up at the sky, which was cloudless.

"We don't even know if there *is* fresh water," she murmured, shaking her head. "It hasn't rained for weeks."

"There *is* water. There has to be water in more than one place, and we'll find it," he said with determination. Both his voice and his hands grew gentler. Perhaps he realized how roughly he had been holding her. The intentness in his gray eyes softened. "We'll find it," he repeated. "I promise you."

The wind tangled her hair and pulled at her clothes. She looked back over her shoulder at the dune where Mr. M. lay and Adrian sat huddled, still sawing at his boot. They had both asked her for water, and she was thirsty, too.

She turned her eyes back to Gabe's solemn face. He no longer looked angry, just serious and unyielding.

"How can you be sure there's water?" she asked, brushing strands of hair back from her face.

For the first time she could remember he smiled without bitterness or mockery. His mouth curved up slightly at one corner. "I'll prove it," he said with an encouraging nod. "Look."

He drew one hand from her shoulder and pointed several yards farther up the beach. A few shells lay strewn on the smooth sand. Around the shells meandered a series of regular markings.

For a moment Whitney stared at them without comprehending their importance. Then her mind raced back over the years to when she had lived in with her grandmother and had trailed along after her uncle Dub. Long ago Dub had taught her what such marks signified.

"Raccoon tracks," she said softly, and in spite of the heat and her weariness, she smiled. Her mind raced; tracks meant, of course, that animals lived on the island, and they couldn't survive without a constant source of fresh water.

Gabe was right. All they had to do was track the raccoon, and they'd find their way to water.

She looked at Gabe with new respect and a sense of reluctant trust. She pushed the sleeves of her green sweater up in determination. She had been born both a worker and a fighter, and she was ready to work and fight now for the ultimate stake—survival.

"All right," she said. "We find water. What then?"

"The first-aid box has water purification tablets, enough to last a couple of days, at least. But the first thing, before we look for water, is to find a campsite."

She looked at him questioningly. "What's wrong with here? Here we could see a boat if one came along. It's an open stretch of beach. People could see us."

"Too open. Feel that sun? The men need shelter. We'll have to move them."

She nodded, biting her lip in concentration. He made sense. "Where?" she asked.

"Into the woods for now," he said without hesitation. "We'll move, then look for water. Later we can look for the ruins of the old Fredericks estate and see what's left. Not much, from what I've heard. But that's on the other side of the island. We may have to locate there eventually. Any boat that comes along will approach from that direction more than likely."

She nodded again, remembering. There had been an estate. It had burned and been neglected, but some part might still stand. Even the humblest shed would protect Mr. Mortalwood better than the forest. And who knew what they might find in the ruins? Any number of things that could help them survive.

"The estate had to have water," she said thoughtfully. "There might even be a well. We'd likely still have to purify the water, but we could solve a lot of problems at one spot—

shelter, water, a better lookout point. There might even be fruit trees or something left...."

He smiled again, a ghost of satire haunting the corners of his mouth. He squeezed her shoulder and released it. "No wonder you're an executive, Shane," he commented. "You *can* do more than look pretty. You think."

She suddenly became too conscious of his touch. It burned her flesh more hotly than the sun, made it tingle more restlessly than the wind. Perhaps he became aware of it, too, for this time when she stepped away from him, his hand dropped away.

She stood for a moment, a wave of cold passing over her in spite of the sunshine. Her clothes had dried in the brisk wind, her hair was nearly dry, and she crossed her arms, trying to gather her strength, her courage and her whirling thoughts.

She would have to depend on Gabe Cantrell as long as they were on the island; there was no question of that. But she must not depend on him too much. She would cooperate, but must keep her independence at all costs.

She took a deep breath of the salt air. She could feel Gabe watching her, and it made her spine prickle, so she tried to ignore him, staring along the shoreline. Far down the beach, she thought she saw something washed up on the sand, and her eyes narrowed with pleasure.

She began walking toward it, as swiftly as she could. The damp sand sucked at her sandals. She heard Gabe's voice behind her. "Where are you going?" he demanded. "You need to explain all this to Mortalwood."

She glanced back at him over her shoulder, a cool look of executive resolve. "You explain. I'm going beachcombing. I see something we might use. And take a look at Adrian's ankle. You're better at bandages than I am."

"Aye, aye," Gabe replied with a maximum amount of sarcasm. She shrugged it off and kept walking. She wanted the unceasing wind to blow away the feel of his hands on her, to wash her clean of the memory of his touch.

He was handsome, he was confident, and he was far from stupid. But he still reminded her of the men back in Kanker County, aimless and without ambition. She had been taught long ago never to desire the touch of such a man.

She had been trained instead to be cautious. And to think.

That was it, she told herself, striding down to the beach. She must think her way through all these problems. Think and never stop thinking. There was no time to feel.

WHITNEY RETURNED to the dune, lugging her treasures and feeling rather pleased with herself. But her pleasure died quickly when she saw that Mr. Mortalwood was unable to stand by himself. He leaned against Gabe, his arm looped heavily around the taller man's neck.

She dropped her things into the reeds and weeds at the sand's edge and ran to his side.

"I can't seem to stand, Whitney," Mr. Mortalwood said when he saw her. He tried to smile, but the smile was lopsided and quickly turned to a mask of pain. "I've pulled something in my back. And my left leg doesn't want to work."

Whitney sucked in a breath, fearful he was more badly hurt than they could tell.

"It's all right," Gabe told him. "I can carry you."

"My boy," Mr. M. said, huffing with pain, "I weigh as much as you do. It'll be too much."

"I can handle it," Gabe said in a tone that brooked no objection. "I just need one thing—two things, really. Your shoes."

"Certainly," Mr. M. said, and managed to slip out of them. Somehow, miraculously, the white yachting shoes hadn't been knocked from his feet during the accident, but now they were stained by water and smudged with sand.

Gabe slipped into them, grimacing a bit at the tight fit, and then, with barely a show of strain, he hoisted the older man into his arms.

"I feel like an idiot," mumbled Mortalwood. Then he grunted with pain, whether from his bruised ribs or his hurt back, Whitney couldn't tell.

Adrian sat sullenly on the dune, staring out to sea. His ankle was expertly bandaged and his left boot had been cut down into a sort of slipper. Gabe must have done it, Whitney thought, remembering Adrian's awkwardness with the knife.

"Do you want me to help you?" she asked Adrian.

"No," he said shortly, not looking at her. "Find me a stick or a staff of some kind. I'll walk by myself."

Whitney didn't like taking orders from Adrian, but she bit her tongue and said nothing. He was in pain and he was frightened, she could tell. If she knew Adrian, however, the thing he was most frightened about was that his dignity had been damaged. That, and the fact his precious deal involving Sand Dollar had been sabotaged by this incident.

Poking among the sea wheat and driftwood, she found a tree branch roughly the size of a cane. It was barkless and polished by the sea. She handed it to him. "How's the ankle?" she asked as civilly as she could.

He struggled painfully to his feet, waving away any assistance she might give. "*He* says it's only sprained," he grumbled. "What does he know? I'd nearly gotten myself loose when *he* came in, panicked and nearly killed me. I was doing fine—until then."

Whitney said nothing. She didn't believe him, but this was no time to argue.

"This is a mistake," Adrian said bitterly. "We shouldn't go inland. We should stay on the shore where we could flag down a boat. That deckhand's head is full of rocks. And Mortalwood's in no shape to make decisions."

"You're already sunburned, Adrian," she said shortly. He was. The wind and sun had pinkened his pale face, and his eyes looked swollen, the lids puffy. His usually perfectly groomed hair was stiff with salt and spiky from the incessant wind.

"I'm going along with this for the time being," Adrian said, turning his back on her. "Mortalwood's too shaken to take charge, so as soon as I rest and get some damned water, *I'm* taking charge of this situation."

With an obviously painful hobbling hop, he made his way after Gabe. Gabe had found some sort of path through the weeds that edged the beach. Whitney could see the naked, brown vee of Gabe's back and the play of his muscles as he carried his heavy burden.

She sighed and pushed her hair from her eyes. If Adrian thought he was going to take control of the party, he had another think coming, she vowed. He could no more find his way around a wild island than he could flap his arms and fly.

Adrian might have seniority over her, but she and Gabe Cantrell would have to make the decisions, and that was that.

She saw Gabe's black-and-white shirt still lying on the dune, where he had put it to pillow Mr. M.'s head. She picked it up, shaking the sand out of it. Kneeling, she spread it out, then gathering the finds from her beachcombing, she wrapped them in the shirt, using it as a crude knapsack.

She picked up the heavy first-aid box in her other arm, threw the strap of her purse over her shoulder, then followed the men down the path that led toward the forest.

Beyond the beach was a low-lying weedy marsh, beyond which the terrain rose and gave way to thickets of pine that reminded Whitney of the places of her childhood, before her mother had come to take her to live in town.

Beyond the pines was a great stand of live oaks, huge tall trees that Whitney was sure were ancient. The live oaks cast a thick, dark shade over the ground, and gray-green beards of Spanish moss swayed from their limbs.

Here, among the oaks, Gabe chose to stop. He set Mr. Mortalwood down on the thick trunk of a fallen tree and told the hobbling Adrian Fisk to watch his step.

Adrian replied acidly that he *was* watching his step. There was bloody cactus all over, he said. His wounded foot, the one with the boot cut low, was already scratched from their spines.

Whitney had been unable to catch up with the others, even the badly limping Adrian, because the first-aid box was heavy, and with her other bundle, her burdens were awkward. She had noticed the cactus immediately and picked her way carefully to avoid it.

Gabe moved forward to meet her, taking the box. "Why are you carrying that?" he demanded. "It's too heavy."

"I can do my share," she objected, but she was panting with the effort, and her arms ached.

He put down the first-aid box beside Adrian, who had sat gingerly on a stump after first inspecting it for insects. "Here, Fisk," Gabe said without friendliness. "Patch up those cactus cuts. You don't want to be any more helpless than you already are."

"Don't think you're giving orders here. You're not," Adrian said coldly. But Gabe ignored him, and Adrian, his face strained with anger, at last opened the box and began to search for balm for his new wounds.

Gabe turned his attention to Whitney. "And what's the executive beachcomber picked up?" he asked sarcastically.

"Your shirt, for one thing," she said, unsmiling.

"Which you've turned into quite the duffel bag. What a good little camper you are."

"Do you want to see what I've got or not?" she asked, chin in the air.

"Sure," he said with a shrug. "Bring it over here." He led her to a large boulder, almost waist high. It had a nearly flat top that made it into a natural table. She set the shirt down and quickly undid the knots.

He stood closely enough beside her that she could feel the heat of his long body. She tried, unsuccessfully, to ignore the power of his physical presence.

"You don't tie a bad knot," he said with grudging admiration. "Do they teach that in vice president's school?"

"My uncle taught me," she replied coolly. Dub, according to Whitney's mother, was good-for-nothing, a shiftless river rat who did little more than fish and hunt. But at least, Whitney thought, he'd liked children, and he'd taught her a thing or two that she'd often found useful.

"I have," Whitney said, unfolding the shirt, "a gallon plastic milk bottle and a two-liter soda-pop bottle. If we find water, we'll need something to carry it in. Voilà."

She gave him a challenging look. His ironic smile stayed in place, but he cocked an appreciative brow. "Not bad thinking," he said, "for a girl."

She shot him an icy look that bounced off him, leaving his self-satisfaction unharmed. "Also," she said, "three aluminum cans—" she produced them with a flourish "—nearly as good as new. We might be able to heat something up in them, if you're brilliant enough to invent fire."

"I'm impressed," he said, not sounding impressed. "What else?"

"This!" she said triumphantly. She drew what appeared to be a jumbled heap of dirty string from the shirt. It was heavy with small, attached weights.

"My God," he said, looking first at her, than at it. He grinned in what seemed real admiration. "Do you know what that is?"

"Yes," Whitney informed him. "It's a casting net. It's torn, but it can be fixed. We can catch fish."

"Don't tell me you can use that thing," he said out of the side of his mouth.

"Yes," she said crisply. "I can." Dub had taught her that, too. It had been years since she'd done it, but casting a net was the sort of elemental skill one didn't forget, like riding a bicycle.

Her green cardigan, ruined and full of sand, still hung limply around her neck. She could unravel its threads and patch the net. She might not do an expert job, but she could do it, and that was what counted.

"Okay," he said. "Now I'll show you something." He leaned his elbow on the rock and dug his hand into his pocket. Whitney wished he still had his shirt on; it was disconcerting always to be dealing with a half-naked man.

"I have every sailor's friend here," he said, watching her face closely. "A waterproof container. Of matches." He showed her a metal vial with a screw top. He opened it. Over two-dozen safety matches lay tucked inside, looking as dry as if they had been stored in the desert.

She smiled at him, wonder in her eyes. He smiled back.

Mortalwood sat on his log, staring blankly into the distance, as if he were in some private world far from all of them.

Adrian, dabbing iodine on his cactus punctures, glowered across the clearing at them. "What are you two doing, standing there grinning across a pile of junk?" he demanded. "Find some water. Set up a signal for help. Do you two realize it might be over a *day* before anybody finds us? We've got to come up with a strategy."

Neither Gabe nor Whitney seemed to hear him.

Laughter played at Gabe's lips, but the light in his eyes was serious and intense. Whitney knew he was trying to take her true measure, just as she was trying to take his.

Earlier that day she had boarded a yacht wearing her best silk suit, proud of her topaz earrings and the fact she had a new Mercedes sedan at home and almost forty thousand dollars in her bank account. She'd been haughty and full of self-importance.

But that had been a different world, and now such things seemed irrelevant, hardly worth thinking of.

This was a new world, dangerous and stripped to essentials. Absent luxuries didn't count. Only survival did.

They had little: containers, a knife, a limited amount of medicine, a few matches, a net to catch food. They knew there was water somewhere and they had the means to make fire. They had little; yet it was a great deal.

"You know what this means?" Gabe asked, nodding ironically at their humble pile of belongings.

"Yes," she said, her chin up. She knew. "We're rich," she said with satisfaction. "That's what it means."

He nodded. "Indeed we are," he said.

Briefly, for only a few seconds, he placed his tanned and scarred hand over her paler one, covering it, squeezing it slightly. The warmth and power of his touch spread like an elixir through her veins.

From the ocean, only half a mile away, came the dull, incessant rumble of waves. As Gabe's hand closed fleetingly over hers, Whitney looked up into his eyes. For a moment her heart rose and soared like one of the birds of the sea. *We can make it together,* she thought.

CHAPTER FOUR

WHITNEY LOOKED AWAY. Gabe quickly took his hand from hers as if he regretted touching her. She tried to marshal her churning thoughts.

"Water," she said mechanically, her voice steady with her best I-mean-business tone. "We've got shelter, crude as it is. But we've got to find water. That's our next priority."

She didn't look at him, but she could hear the sarcasm in his reply. "Aye, aye. My thoughts exactly, sir."

She whipped her head around to face him, her expression severe. "Don't call me *sir*. This is serious."

He stood, one hip cocked, his arms crossed languidly across his chest. The breeze from the sea was slowed and softened by the pines and live oaks, but she could still hear the boom of the waves, and the mossy beards of the oaks stirred sleepily in the salt-kissed air.

"Yes, sir," he said, and raised a lazy hand to stroke the stubble of his jaw. He regarded her calmly, his eyes narrowed slightly.

Don't lose control, Whitney thought with a passion she knew better than to show. She had, after all, Mr. M. and Adrian Fisk to take care of; she didn't need to waste her energy clashing with Gabe Cantrell, no matter how provoking he was.

"All right," she said with elaborate composure. "Call me whatever amuses you. I couldn't care less. But we need water. That means tracking the raccoon. I'll do that, and you stay here and take care of the men."

He actually blinked in surprise. "*You'll* track? Excuse me—*you* stay here and play nurse. I'll go after the raccoon."

She drew herself up to her full height, and even though she still had to look up at him, it made her feel as tall as he was. "The person best qualified for the job should do the job," she said in her most managerial manner.

He put one hand on his hip and gave her a crooked grin of disbelief. "*You're* the best qualified to track a raccoon?" He shook his head in dubious amusement.

"To my knowledge," Whitney said coolly. "So *you* stay and play nurse, Cantrell. I'll be back as soon as I can." She picked up the empty gallon jug and the two-liter bottle. "Keep the men comfortable. Mr. Mortalwood's aspirins are in his shirt pocket. He's already had two."

She turned and called over her shoulder, "I'm going to find you water, Mr. M. Don't worry. We're going to be fine."

She started to stride away, toward the rough path that led to the beach.

"Hold it," Gabe Cantrell growled, catching her by the elbow. "You may be hot stuff in the boardroom, lady, but don't try giving *me* orders. I'll do the tracking. I know how. You may know how to follow the stock market. It's not the same as following an animal."

Whitney jerked her arm away, giving him her most regal stare. Despite her outer coolness, her heart rapped against her ribs, and she wished he wasn't half-naked, clad only in those low-riding white shorts.

"Then we'll both go," she said, steel in her voice. "If you're . . . adequate, then I'll trust you at it after this. Until then, Mr. Cantrell, you're an unproven quantity."

His coppery brows drew together in a frown of incredulity. "You're asking me to prove myself?" he said with a snide crook to his mouth.

"Precisely." Whitney turned and spoke over her shoulder again. "Mr. M., we've *both* decided to look for water. Adrian, you can hold the fort while we're gone, can't you?"

Mr. Mortalwood nodded as amiably as he could, and Adrian, sitting miserably on his stump, shot her a look that was meant to kill. He didn't bother to answer. He only glared.

She ignored it. She would deal with Adrian's attitude later, when she had the luxury of time. She looked up at Gabe, who was watching her with what seemed a mixture of skepticism and mockery.

"Come along, if you're coming," she said to him, and set off down the weedy path.

"Aye, aye, sir," he said again, shrugging his bare shoulders and following her lackadaisically. He picked up his shirt, but didn't bother to put it on.

Don't call me sir, she wanted to order again, clenching her fists to show him she meant business. But she knew that to show such a response would please him, and she wouldn't give him the satisfaction.

Keeping her back straight, she stayed in the lead, making her way purposefully toward the beach, trying to pay no attention to him.

But as the boom and hiss of the surf grew nearer, she kept remembering, against her will, that for one insane moment she had lain in his arms, and it had felt like a sort of deliverance for which she had waited her whole life.

HE WAS BETTER than she was, drat it. She hated with all her heart to admit it, but she was, above all, a realist. Conceding that she had once again underestimated him stung like salt in a wound.

His expression sardonic, he had let her follow the raccoon's path on the damp sand of the beach where tracking was easy.

He had kept silent while she looked for the raccoon's trail in the woods. Dub had taught her years ago that wild animals often followed surprisingly routine courses. "Mr. Possum, Mr. Coon, even Mr. Mouse—all's creatures of habit. You look careful for where the weeds're all tromped down. That's a road."

But when the pines begin to thicken and the weeds to thin, Whitney stopped, confused and uncertain of which way the animal had gone.

Gabe allowed her only a moment of hesitation. "That way," he said, stepping in front of her for the first time. He nodded toward a weed that was bent ever so slightly the wrong way.

Grudgingly Whitney followed. He was good, damn him. He was as good as Dub himself had been.

And she was out of practice, she thought in frustrated rationalization. Besides that, she hadn't spent that many years under Dub's tutelage. Her mother had come for her and taken her to town, telling her to forget such skills. They were useless, worthless, lower class.

Eager to please, Whitney had learned new skills, the sort her mother valued. But now, over the years, her mind and heart yearned for Dub and all he had known. She willed herself to remember everything he had taught her, everything.

"There," Gabe said harshly. He pointed at a large, lichen-covered rock under the shadow of a tall, gnarled pine.

He stopped, and so did she. She narrowed her eyes, holding her breath, straining to see what he saw.

Then, suddenly, she realized that one side of the rock was damp. She knelt softly by it and took a closer look. A tiny spring bubbled up at the stone's base, creating little more than a tiny puddle. The thirsty earth had drunk all other trace of it.

She raised her eyes and met Gabe's unsettling, steady gray stare. He had found it more quickly and efficiently than she could have.

She thought he would smirk at her, but he did not. Instead, he crossed his arms over his chest and looked her up and down. "You're not half-bad," he said, his head cocked slightly as he seemed to take her measure.

You're the one who's impressive, she could have said. But she would not offer him a compliment. He stood there unsmiling in the dappled light that fell through the pines, and he reminded her more than ever of a golden-haired savage, a man from a world far more elemental than her own.

"It's a slow spring," she said shortly. "These bottles won't be easy to fill."

"We'll both work at it." He reached over and took the jug from her. His fingers brushed hers, barely touching them, but the contact sent a tiny shudder thrilling through her. Quickly, involuntarily, she took a half step back, then regretted it. He was, she realized instinctively, a man to whom it was dangerous to show weakness.

Slowly, his eyes still challenging hers, he smiled his crooked smile. Her heart seemed to freeze into stillness, then suddenly burn.

Turning from him, she began to fill the bottle, stopping to shake the water in it, trying to rinse it thoroughly of the salt of the sea.

Wordlessly he knelt beside her, his bare shoulder almost touching her sweatered one. She willed herself to work coolly and not to flinch at his nearness. She tried to center all her concentration on filling the bottle, not on his presence, a presence that was so close she could feel the heat radiating from his nearly naked torso.

"Can you really use that net?" he asked at last, his voice low, almost rasping.

She stared at the slowly filling bottle instead of looking at him. "Yes," she answered shortly. "I just don't know what there's to catch. I don't know much about the ocean."

"Mullet," he said just as shortly, "and shrimp. In the shallows. There's also a small tidal river that runs into the island. When the tide's right, that'd be the surest place."

"When's the tide right?"

"It's best high."

"Which is it now?"

"It's about done going out."

Whitney, her bottle filled, rose, frowning. "When's it high again?"

He, too, rose, the jug in his hand dripping with clear water. He put purification tablets in each container of water. "About twelve hours."

She found herself staring at the small blue alligator tattooed on his chest, grinning from its forest of blond hairs. Disconcerted, she looked away. "Well, I can't wait that long. Mr. Mortalwood needs food. So does Adrian. They both need to build their strength."

"There's plenty of food around," he assured her with sarcasm. "You just have to know where to look."

Her eyes snapped upward to lock with his. "I'm quite aware of that," she said with equal sarcasm. "And I happen to know where to look. There must be squirrels in these trees," she said, waving her hand toward the overhanging branches. "And there might be ducks or something out in the water. There might even be deer . . ."

"There are," he said smugly. "I saw a track."

Blast! Whitney thought. How had she missed it? He shrugged nonchalantly and turned back toward their camp. "Watch your step," he said, sounding bored. "You're getting scratched by the cactus and burrs. You won't be any good to me if you can't walk. You've got to watch every step you take here. There are snakes—"

"I'm not in the least afraid of snakes," Whitney said. She had killed a copperhead with a hoe when she was only eight.

She hurried after Gabe, being more careful, however, to watch her step than before. "We could catch a squirrel or a duck or a deer if we had a gun," she mused. "But we don't. We don't even have anything to make a trap."

He kept on walking, taking long-legged strides that she found hard to keep up with. "Don't need a trap."

"Look," Whitney said, "if you're one of those people who thinks a person can live on cattails and tree bark, think again, because Mr. Mortalwood is not used to—"

He cast a dubious glance at her. "What am I supposed to do? Pull a filet mignon and a magnum of champagne out of my hat? I don't even have a hat, dammit."

The breeze from the sea tossed his sun-streaked hair over his brow, giving him a lighthearted air that the set of his mouth belied. She took his slight pause as a chance to catch up with him. She intended to stay at his side if it killed her.

She winced as another cactus attacked her bare ankle. "I mean it," she said, trying to ignore the sting. "He can't. Eat cattails and treebark or something horrid like that."

He exhaled sharply, as if bored with her. "It's not really the right season for cattails—and I can do better than tree bark. Do you know you have a cactus sticking out of your ankle, *Miss* Shane?"

"So what?" Whitney retorted. "Just keep walking. I can keep up."

He stopped, turning to her. "Not for long. You're bleeding. Look, don't try to prove you're tough. You've already proved it."

She was surprised that he dropped to his knee before her and carefully removed the piece of cactus. He even poured a bit of the precious water in his hand and rubbed the drops of blood away. His touch was surprisingly gentle and the water felt deliciously cooling.

"Just how you've always wanted me," he grumbled, cleaning the wound with another handful of water. "Kneeling at your feet. I mean it, watch where you step."

He rose abruptly, and she found that they were standing closer to each other than she had expected. Once more she was looking at the alligator smirking from its forest of blond hair. She swallowed hard and forced herself not to step back.

"What are those things, anyway?" she asked, frowning at the low-lying cactus that grew everywhere. They were squat, dark, ugly plants that seemed to consist of nothing except small, vicious clusters of spines. Each cluster could detach itself from the main plant and stick like a burr.

He didn't say anything for a moment. The crash and sigh of the surf was closer now, its primal rhythm echoing.

"They're called jumping cactus," he said at last, turning away from her again and moving on. "That's what they do. If you get too close, they practically jump on you, and then jump to some other part of your leg if you so much as brush them. The devil invented them on a particularly off day."

Once more Whitney hurried to keep off, but this time she made sure she kept her eyes on the ground. The evil little cacti did seem programmed to leap on any hapless passerby.

She was relieved when she and Gabe reached the shore again, where the hard-packed gray sand was free of burrs and cacti and tripping vines.

But Gabe wasn't heading toward camp; he moved down the beach in the opposite direction. "Where are we going?" she asked. "The camp's the other way. Are you lost?"

He tossed her a glance and laughed without real humor. He was, she realized, laughing at her. "Lost? Me? Not quite. There's a river marsh down here," he said. "We'll find some mussels for lunch."

"Mussels?" Whitney said, wrinkling her nose in distaste. "River mussels?" She had seen plenty of river mussels as a child. Dub said they tasted like mud and were fit only for raccoons to eat.

"These are different. Europeans often eat them. Do you want to see how this is done? Or do you need to carry water back to your Mr. M.? Can you find your way? Or are *you* lost?"

"I have an *excellent* sense of direction," Whitney responded. The wind was always high along the beach, and it made her hair stream behind her. Her navy slacks flapped hard against her thighs, and the heat of the sun forced her to untie her ruined cardigan from her neck to carry it.

When Gabe stopped to take off his shoes, she was unable to resist imitating him and bent to take off her navy leather sandals. The damp sand felt delicious beneath her feet, sending a soft rush of coolness up through her body.

Overhead the gulls dipped and glided, and an occasional brown pelican soared through the air on its mighty wings. Farther down the shore, in a small bay, myriad water birds had gathered, wading, flying and stitching the wind with their shrill cries.

Whitney took a deep breath of salt air and edged closer to the surf, so that the froth of the incoming waves would eddy over her feet. In contrast to the beating sun, its coolness felt almost icy. *So this is what the ocean's really like,* she thought with a surge of wonder.

The water glittered brilliantly in the afternoon light, mostly gray, but touched here and there by areas of blue that mirrored the azure sky. Its sound never ceased; it was like the breathing of some immense and powerful creature.

For a moment she could almost forget her cares about Mr. Mortalwood and Adrian and lose herself in the cleanness of the air and the unspoiled beauty of the sea and the shore.

"You look almost dreamy. Planning how many condos to put up on this stretch of beach?" Gabe's voice had a harsh and jarring note to it.

She blinked in displeased surprise. "No," she said emphatically. "I wasn't. Why should I think of condos?"

"Because that's your business, isn't it? Isn't it what Mortalwood does in Atlanta? That's why the interest in the island, scouting it, the maps, the photos—isn't it?"

"Not in the least," she lied, resenting his insight. He had guessed exactly why they had taken this ill-advised trip to Sand Dollar. He was too observant, his powers of deduction and intuition too good. It unnerved her.

She felt another foreign and wholly unexpected sensation as well: guilt. Now that she had seen the beauty of the beach and the island's interior, she knew the Mortalwood Corporation would buy Sand Dollar. They would be rescued, business would go on as usual, and they would be foolish not to acquire the island. And once they had it, the only logical course would be to develop it for all it was worth.

"Want to tell me exactly what the three of you are up to?" Gabe asked, his eyes narrowed against the glare of the sun.

She glanced at him covertly. He resembled a gilded barbarian, perfectly at home on this deserted shore. His hair danced in the wind like a pale flame.

"What we're doing is . . . confidential," she said. The answer sounded rude, but it wasn't her fault; she couldn't tell him their intentions even if she wanted to.

"I see," he said, smiling mirthlessly. "I can fetch, carry, find water and feed you. But I shouldn't ask questions. You don't give answers."

She ran her hand uneasily through her blowing hair. "You can ask all the questions you want. But no—I don't give answers." She tried to make her answer sound airily polite, but final. She feared the attempt at politeness had failed miserably.

She tried again. "Why don't you let me ask you some questions for a change?" she said, trying again to sound light. "What are those things?" She pointed to the ridged seashells that littered the beach everywhere.

"Cockleshells," he said shortly.

"And those, the bigger, twisted ones," she persisted.

"Whelks. And if you see one trying to stand on its head, grab it. It means it's alive and trying to burrow into the sand. They're edible."

Whitney smiled in spite of herself, and her sharp eyes scanned the beach all the more intently. "Oh—and this?" She picked up a small, shiny shell, almost bullet-shaped.

"It's called an olive, but forget it, you can't eat 'em."

Whitney slipped the smooth little shell into her pocket, anyway. She had never been on an unspoiled beach before. She had never, in fact, found an unbroken seashell before. "What's that?" she asked, picking up another one, disk-shaped, and tinged with a delicate gold.

"A moon shell," he said impatiently. "You can't eat that, either."

Whitney didn't care. She slipped that shell, too, into her pocket. "Oh, look—isn't that a sand dollar?" she asked, pointing toward a brown, dull shell shaped like a flat biscuit.

"Yes," he muttered, "and that's a jellyfish you're about to step on in your bare feet." He seized her by the shoulders and steered her around the jellyfish, a quivering translucent shape that looked like a deflating, ghostly balloon.

Whitney's heart leapt in alarm, but it leapt, as well, at Gabe's unexpected touch. He released her almost immediately, as if he had regretted the contact. "Are you going to gather seashells?" he asked out of the corner of his mouth, "or are you going to help feed the helpless and hapless back there at camp?"

Whitney, hurt, forgot about the sand dollar. She had tried to be friendly in a civil, impersonal sort of way. He had rejected her.

When they reached the estuary of the river that led into the marsh, he stopped her. He set down the jug of water and his shoes, put his hands on his hips and gazed thoughtfully at her. "All right. It gets a little messy now," he said. "Watch. I'll show you how it's done in case you ever have to do it yourself. But it means getting muddy."

He went wading into the mud. Whitney looked after him as he made his way slowly through the reeds and tall, green grasses. She was both a competitive person and a capable one and didn't like being left behind. She set down her bottle and her sandals, rolled up the legs of her slacks and went in right after him. She tried to watch the tanned vee of his back and the black mud of the marsh at the same time.

The mud oozed up over her feet like liquid velvet, but she gritted her teeth and kept going. She'd slogged through mud before as a child, and it hadn't kill her. It wouldn't kill her now.

He turned and his brows went up slightly when he saw her making her way behind him. "Hey!" he protested. "I told you to stay put. This is muddy."

"I'm not afraid of mud," Whitney said with spirit, pulling her foot from the sucking marsh and taking a cautious step forward. "If one person can find mussels, two people can find twice as many."

He stared at her, a smile slowly forming on his lips. "Thinking like management again, Miss Shane? Efficiency and productivity? No wasted man—or woman—power?"

She forged on, her chin raised. "Thinking like a hungry person, Mr. Cantrell. We've got a job to do. Let's do it."

He paused, shaking his head, waiting for her to catch up to him. In truth, the mud did make her feel a bit squeamish, but she refused to let fear or distaste stop her.

He crossed his arms so that for a moment the blue 'gator was hidden. "I've got to hand it to you, Shane," he said, shaking his head again. "You're something."

Her foot sank so deeply into the mud that she almost lost her balance. His arm streaked out and caught her by the shoulder, keeping her upright.

For a moment they stood that way, his hand clamped on her, making sure she had her balance. He looked into her eyes, and she looked into his. They were like two opponents, carefully measuring each other.

Or they were like two companions, bound together, studying each other in hopes of finding how deeply, how completely, they might trust each other.

He released her shoulder and looked down at her feet, black with marsh mud. "You're something, all right," he breathed again.

Suddenly, for one absurd instant, Whitney forgot her multitude of troubles and felt a strange surge of happiness.

But their situation on the island was so serious that the moment faded almost as swiftly as it had appeared.

The two of them turned their eyes away as if they had never touched each other or searched each other's eyes so intently. If she didn't know better, she would think he was as temporarily at a loss for words as she was.

GABE WAS RIGHT. Gathering mussels was not a job for the fastidious. Her feet were muddy, and her hands were muddy past the wrists, for the mussels liked to burrow into the shallows of the black mud and had to be pried out. She had streaked her slacks with mud, her green sweater was freckled with splashes of it, and her fingernails felt as if they might never be clean again.

But she had filled her cardigan with almost as many mussels as Gabe had managed to dig out and carry in his shirt. They waded back through the thicker mud that ringed the mussel bed, and then each took one economical drink of water, leaving dark handprints on the jug. They looked at their handprints and at each other and stifled wry smiles.

The sun beat down on them. Whitney was almost headachy with heat, but anxious to get back to Mr. M. and Adrian. She estimated that she and Gabe had been gone for upward of an hour, probably more. Mr. M. would be worried, and both he and Adrian would be uncomfortable. Still, she smiled when she thought of Adrian trying to gather mussels. He would starve to death before he walked into the mud.

When they reached the beach again, the wind had picked up. Whitney's hair began to fly about her face, and she had no choice but to brush it back with her mud-caked hand.

"Come on," Gabe said, putting down his shirt, shoes and water jug, before taking Whitney's from her. "We both look those Mudmen of New Guinea that they show on the *Na-*

tional Geographic specials. Let's get in the ocean and clean up.''

Whitney shook her head. ''Later. We need to get back to Mr. M.'

''Mr. M.'s blood pressure'll soar off the chart if he sees you like that,'' Gabe said with cheerful contempt. ''He'll have a heart attack. He'll think the swamp hag's come for him.''

Whitney wavered. She supposed they did look filthy and ghastly, perhaps frighteningly so.

''Come on,'' Gabe repeated, and started wading into the sea. ''It won't take a minute.''

Reluctantly, she waded after him, pausing when she was waist deep to scrub her hands. He was farther out, swimming, diving beneath the water and coming up, shaking the water away so that his hair flashed like gold.

He dove and surfaced almost beside her, spattering her when he shook his head. ''Oh, come on,'' he said in disgust. ''Get into it.''

''This is fine,'' Whitney said primly, concentrating on getting her hands clean.

He stood beside her. The seawater streamed off his chest and shoulders. ''No,'' he said firmly. ''It isn't. It doesn't do anything about the mud on your face.''

''On my face?'' Whitney asked unhappily, although she supposed it had been inevitable. ''Where?'' She began to splash the water rather fussily at her face.

''For a girl who swims like a 'gator, you wash like a pussycat,'' he said with a mocking smile. He bent over her and ran his wet hand gently down her cheek. He did it repeatedly, sluicing away the last signs of the marsh.

''Good grief,'' he said with distaste. ''You've even got it in your ear.''

"Ow!" Whitney said, as he scrubbed vigorously at her ear, but she had to laugh, too.

"And you've got flakes of the stuff in your hair," he admonished her. "The only way you'll ever be clean is to get into the water completely. Take a deep breath."

"I can..." ...*do it myself,* she started to protest, but he already had her in his arms.

"*Deep* breath," he warned again, and from the laughing glint in his eye she realized she had no choice. His arm muscles tensed around her, pulling her more securely to him as he braced himself to carry her underwater. She gulped her lungs full of air and without thinking wound her arms around his neck.

He dove with her against an oncoming wave and she hung on to him with all her might, gasped when they surfaced, then let him bear them into the next swell. He did it again and again, until she was dizzy, even giddy.

At last, almost as breathless as she, he stood again, one arm still locked around her. Her feet found the slanting, sandy bottom.

"Are you presentable?" he teased. "Let's see those ears." He inspected her ears carefully and nodded approval. "The hair?" He ran his hands over it, through it, and over it again, smoothing out the water and tangles. "Hair fine," he approved.

"Face?" he said, tilting hers up to his.

The light on his hair was so intense it dazzled her, as if she found herself in the arms of a sun god with a corona of gold about his face. If she lowered her eyes, she would be staring at the bright hair of his chest glistening against the almost mahogany brown of his skin.

The ocean pushed and pulled at her lower body and seemed to be sucking the sandy floor from beneath her, trying to draw her deeper into the water's vast rhythm. Her arms, she found, were still around his neck. She was slightly chilled from the sea, but his flesh was warm, almost hot beneath hers.

He had bent close to examine her face, and he had been smiling. Now, his smile faded, but his hands still cupped her chin.

The cautious, studious look came into his eyes again, and Whitney found her body, which a moment before had been deliciously limp and languid, suddenly tingling with apprehension.

"The face," he said softly, "is fine, too."

Slowly, almost reluctantly, he lowered his mouth to hers.

CHAPTER FIVE

GABE'S MOUTH BRUSHED HERS as the waves thundered and seethed against the shore. He drew her closer, holding her more firmly against him, so securely that even the sea, with all its power, could not pull her from him.

The water surged about Whitney's waist, tugging at her, but she was more conscious of the power of the arms that held her, of the softness of her breasts compressed by the hard warmth of his chest. Her thin sweater felt cold and skimpy and sodden, almost like no barrier at all between their flesh, and the heat of his body seemed to pour into hers in a throbbing, direct current.

His lips hovered above hers, as if both questioning and resisting. For a moment Whitney kept her face raised to his, her eyes shut, for she felt half faint with desire so long repressed that now it seemed to wash over her more irresistibly than any torrent. The edges of her consciousness dimmed, and rational thought spiraled away into a black nothingness. Her body swayed against his, wanting to be swept away by the dark tide of his touch.

His mouth descended purposefully, beginning to take hers with hungry challenge, daring her to share the flood of feeling. *No,* Whitney thought, her reason rushing back, coupled with an unreasoning surge of panic.

What they said about drowning people was true, she thought with terrified wonder. Her life *did* seem to flash disjointedly before her eyes. Everything her mother had sacrificed, everything she herself had labored for and accomplished, every real and grueling episode spun through her mind, clashing with the present moment.

"No!" she cried, pulling away from him vehemently. She almost lost her footing when a swell of waves struck her, but when Gabe reached out to steady her, she pushed his hand away, staggered, but kept her balance by herself.

"No," she repeated. "Don't you ever *dare* do that again."

He was taller and stronger than she, and it was easier for him to keep his balance when the force of the waves hit. The water rushed around him, eddying almost as high as his hips.

Anger mingled with disgust on his face. His eyes narrowed more than usual, and he smiled his unamused smile, one corner of his mouth higher than the other.

"Don't dare?" he drawled, mocking her righteous tone. "You mean, 'Keep my place,' don't you? Not to try anything with my betters?"

Whitney tossed her wet hair back. "Interpret it any way you want," she said from between gritted teeth. "Just because we're stuck in the wilderness doesn't mean I want to play 'You Tarzan, Me, Jane.' Keep that in mind—and that's an *order.*"

She started moving back toward the shore, muscles straining against the push and undertow of the waves. Not looking back, she kept her eyes fixed steadily on the dunes.

"Who gives the orders around here may become an interesting matter before all this is over," she heard him challenge, something very like a sneer in his voice.

She ignored him and kept wading. What was the matter with her? she thought in disgust. He was little more than a deckhand, but she'd been wallowing in his arms like some love-hungry idiot. It was insane.

Was she simply so exhausted and confused and frightened by the day's events that her psyche had yearned briefly for physical comforting, the luxury of leaning for once on someone else's strength? She didn't know, and she refused to think about it. She had too many other things to manage.

When she reached the firm, cool sand of the beach, she sat on a piece of driftwood and put on her sandals. She paid no attention to Gabe when he slogged through the shin-deep water and finally reached the shore. She gathered up her bundle of mussels and bottle of water and set off toward camp, not bothering to wait for him or speak to him.

"You took your time," Adrian said resentfully when she appeared in the small clearing among the live oaks. "Stopped off to have a little swim, I see. While Mr. M. here is practically dehydrating from thirst."

Impatiently Whitney brushed her drying hair out of her eyes. "Here's water and food," she said, setting down the cardigan full of mussels. "Getting it was dirty work. I washed off."

He deserved no apology, but she gave him one, anyway. She knew he was frustrated, in pain, and probably more frightened than he'd ever been in his life. Her tone gentled. "I didn't mean to cause you concern, Adrian."

How horrible, she thought sickly as the reality of their situation sank in again. She was used to seeing an immaculate Adrian sitting at his custom-made desk or in the big conference room. Now he was battered, dirty, powerless, and sitting on a tree stump.

His ankle was badly swollen, his clothing rumpled, torn and dirty, his eyes seemed puffy, and his jaw, where Gabe had been forced to strike him, had turned an ugly, lumpy blue. His split lower lip had swelled, too, giving his mouth a grotesque shape.

She knelt beside Mr. Mortalwood to offer him water. The older man slumped miserably on the fallen log, looking as if he hadn't moved since they'd left him. He took the bottle and drank from it greedily.

Out of the corner of her eye, Whitney saw Adrian Fisk watching jealously, as if he begrudged Mr. M. every swallow.

We'll need water for drinking and cooking and trying to stay clean, Whitney thought with gloomy realism. *I'll have to run back and forth to that spring all day long.*

"Do you want another aspirin?" she asked Mr. Mortalwood with concern, and he nodded feebly. His color was not good, still far too pale, and his eyes had a puzzled, unfocused look. She cursed inwardly that he'd lost his glasses. The poor man could only see this hostile new world as a blur.

She fumbled in his pocket and gave him two more aspirin. He took them gratefully, sucking down several more swallows of the precious water.

"He's not the only one who's thirsty," Adrian complained from behind her.

Silently Whitney handed him the bottle and put her hand on Mr. Mortalwood's forehead, trying to see if he had a fever. His skin felt cold and clammy.

"How do you intend to cook those mussels?" Adrian demanded. "Are you *sure* you can eat those things? And we need more water than this."

She glanced over at him. "They eat them in Europe," she said shortly, unaware of the irony that she was parroting Gabe's words. Adrian, she noted, had drained the bottle. Her mouth was dry. She had taken only one swallow herself. "There's more water on the way," she added, trying to keep her voice even and neutral.

How she was going to fix the mussels without a real cooking vessel she didn't know, but she would think of a way. She had to.

"I've been seeing that we got some *real* food," Adrian said. "I managed to gather a bunch of acorns from these live oaks. Once you get those mussels cooking, you can gather more and help crack them."

"Not unless you want to be sick as a dog, Fisk." Gabe Cantrell had appeared at the clearing's edge. He held the jug at his side by its handle and had the shirtful of mussels tossed carelessly over one bare shoulder.

He moved closer to the group and set his bundle down beside Whitney's. She had not noticed before how quietly his lean body could move.

"What are you talking about?" Adrian demanded, his dark eyes flashing resentment. His hair stood up in black spikes around his angular face, making him look all the more bristling.

"Eat those, pal," Gabe said, with a careless nod toward the tiny pile of acorns, "and you're going to be in major trouble. They're not like regular acorns. They may not kill you, but you'll wish you were dead."

Adrian tried to draw himself up taller, but winced at the effort. He stayed slouched, but his glare was unabated. "How do *you* know?"

Gabe shrugged one naked shoulder. "Don't believe me," he said without concern. "Eat them and see." He turned to Whitney and held the jug out to her. "Here. Drink. A place like this fools you. You can get dehydrated before you know it."

He was the only one of the three men who had thought of her thirst, she noted, half grateful, half resenting that he'd been the one.

She still knelt by Mr. Mortalwood, but she didn't reach for the jug. "Have you drunk?" she asked, her gaze meeting Gabe's without wavering.

"After you," he said, still holding it toward her.

She sensed more than simple concern or consideration in the offer. Her highly tuned senses recognized the subtlest sort of power play.

She shook her head. "No," she answered flatly. "You first."

They stared at each other for a moment charged with confrontation. At last he smiled. "Is that an order?" He raised one blond brow cynically.

"Call it that if you like," Whitney replied with no emotion.

"If the two of you are going to stand there and argue about it, pass it here," Adrian said testily. "I swallowed about a gallon of seawater. My throat still burns."

"Wait for your turn, Fisk," Gabe answered, his voice calm, but his eyes still locked defiantly on Whitney's. Without another word he raised the jug to his lips and took four long swallows.

He wiped the jug's mouth thoroughly with his hand, then extended it to her again. This time she accepted it. Pointedly she wiped it again and took, as he had done, exactly four swallows.

Then she passed the jug to Adrian, who tipped it up and tried to drink so fast that he spilled a good bit of it, sending it pouring across his face.

"Easy, Fisk," Gabe warned. "You can make yourself sick that way, too."

Lawrence Mortalwood stirred, and when Whitney reached to feel his forehead again, he took her hand and held on to it as tightly as if he were a child. "Whitney," he said, looking more confused than before, "I'm hungry. Did you say you brought food?"

"Yes, Mortalwood," Gabe said before she could answer. "We've just got to fix it."

He glanced almost idly around the clearing until his gaze settled on a flat, square rock about the size of a desktop dictionary.

"Feel up to digging, Fisk?" he asked, picking up the rock. "If you do, I can take care of other things. We need a hole about two feet square and a foot and a half feet deep."

"I most certainly *don't* feel like digging," Adrian retorted. "I think I've chipped a bone in my elbow. I can barely move it. You do it."

"Fine." Gabe inspected the clearing again, selected a spot where the ground looked softest, knelt and began to dig, using a corner of the rock.

The earth was difficult to dig, however, and the tool crude and blunt. Gabe grimaced slightly at the effort, and the muscles in his arms snaked and roped. He glanced up at Whitney. "As for you," he suggested, a tinge of sarcasm in his voice, "I suggest you go back to the shore and clean your part of the mussels. They're muddy. Remember? It's only a suggestion, mind you. I wouldn't presume to give an order. If you'd rather I'd do it, you can take over the digging."

Whitney glowered at him and gave Mr. Mortalwood's hand a comforting squeeze. But Gabe wasn't looking at her. He was grimacing again as he threw all his strength into driving the stone into the earth like a blunt blade.

The person who watched her was Adrian. His voice and the expression on his face surprised her. "Do as he says, Whitney. You can't expect Mr. Mortalwood to eat muddy food. Or any of us, for that matter."

She kept her own face stolid and emotionless. Gabe was right, of course, but she hated to acknowledge the fact; she should have thought of washing the mussels. But she had been too upset, too eager to escape him—she, the manager's manager, the woman known for her unflappable efficiency.

She rose with all the dignity she could muster and took up the bundle of mussels again. She didn't take it because Adrian told her to. She did it because it was the only logical, practical thing to do. She certainly couldn't dig the unyielding earth with a stone.

She stood for a moment, pointedly ignoring Adrian to send him the message that he was not her lord and master. Instead, she stared coldly down at Gabe, at his bent head with its wind-tossed hair, his burnished back with its straining muscles.

"I'll be back soon, Mr. M.," she said as cheerily as she could. "We're starting supper right now."

"Yes, yes," he said absently, nodding more to himself than her. "Fine, fine."

Carefully, watching out for the treacherous jumping cacti and their fellow-torturers, the sand burrs, she made her way back to the sea.

She set her jaw grimly, vowing that Gabe Cantrell would never ruin the smooth, machinelike flow of her thoughts again. Still, she was bothered. As the only able-bodied member of Mr. Mortalwood's threesome, she needed to stay in charge.

But Adrian and Gabe were already jousting for control, and she had no illusions; Gabe knew far more about survival than Adrian did or ever would. And Adrian desired ascendancy not only over Gabe but over herself. She could not allow that. She was better able to make decisions in this situation than he, and she knew it.

There was a serious power struggle in the making, and she had to keep her head. She must not alienate Adrian, for she had to work with him when they got out of all of this. But it was Cantrell that she had to trust for the time being. In this emergency, they all needed his strength and knowledge. But she refused to meekly follow his bidding.

Her head ached with the thousand complexities of their dilemma. She would solve the problems one at a time, and not let their numbers overwhelm her. Right now, she had mussels to clean, and clean them she would. She would muddle her mind with nothing else.

As she stepped onto the sandy beach, she was struck by how weary she was, how worn out by the day's events. Suddenly, however, an eerie feeling seized her. The wind was high, the sky deep blue, the sea vast and utterly lonely.

From one edge of the horizon to the other, from one end of the beach to the other, she was the only human. In the distance gulls circled and dived, and occasionally a pelican crossed the sky. But she might have been the only human being on earth, the first or the last.

The sea thundered, and she felt humbled by its immensity, its ceaseless ebb and flow. She was sure of only one thing. In its wild way, it was beautiful, so beautiful it made her ache. And she was alone in it.

No, she amended. She was not alone. There were others back in their crude camp. But oddly, whether from fatigue or the unfamiliarity of the scene before her, she found it difficult to remember what Mr. Mortalwood and Adrian Fisk looked like, or rather, what they looked like when things were normal.

The only image that came clearly to mind was Gabe, bent over the unrelenting earth, determined to best it with the crudest of implements.

The stone savage, she thought, her eyes on the empty horizon, her ears filled with the drumming of the surf. Back there, in the shadows of the giant live oaks, waiting for her, the stone savage.

SHE HAD TO ADMIT that Gabe knew exactly what he was doing. She returned to camp to find he'd dug a crude pit and lined it with rocks. Beside it, he'd started a small but strong fire. With his pocketknife, he'd sliced a heap of wild onions and mushrooms—when he'd found them, Whitney didn't know.

While the fire burned down, he quickly built two lean-to's near the fire, using nothing more than his knife. One shelter was larger than the other, and both were crude. Still, as he constructed the frames, using forked limbs and notched poles, she had to admire the ease and speed with which he worked.

Without being asked, she went to his side to gather pine boughs to cover the frames. "Nobody asked you to help," he said out of the side of his mouth. "Sit down. Rest."

Whitney, struggling to twist off a particularly stubborn bough, tossed him a cool look. "As long as you work, I work. What do we do after this?"

He came to her side, reached for the bough and wrenched it away with one powerful movement, letting it fall into her hands. "You're asking me? I thought you liked to give the orders."

Without missing a beat, Whitney set down the bough in a heap she'd gathered and began to wrestle another. "Listen," she said in her best no-nonsense voice, "you obviously know more about this kind of thing than the rest of us—"

"Flattery?" he asked ironically, snapping the bough off for her. He put one hand on his chest so it covered the small blue alligator. "Be still, my heart."

"I'm not flattering you, I'm stating a fact," Whitney said, moving on to another pine. "You've got knowledge. We'd be foolish not to use it."

He let her pull, jiggle and jerk on the limb, turning calmly to another tree. "Ah," he said, a chiding merriment in his voice, "I see. The good little executive consults experts in fields foreign to her and delegates authority. I'm being *allowed* to take charge for a while, is that it?"

"Put it however you like," she said, tossing her hair from her eyes. In frustration, she picked up a small sharp stone and began to hack at the recalcitrant branch. Her blows were awkward but effective. The pale wood began to show beneath the pierced bark. *Oh, heavens,* she thought in disgust. *I'm becoming a stone savage myself.*

"And you," she added, pounding at the branch, "answered a question with a question. That's not polite. I said, what do we do next? After we've got enough of these blasted limbs?"

He turned and cocked his head, watching her hammer and cut at the branch with the rock. He gave her the kind of look a man might give to a clever dog who had just learned a new trick. "Look at that. It's learned to use tools. It's inventing the ax."

Whitney glared darkly at the branch and gritted her teeth to keep from saying something rude. If she was indeed a savage and not civilized, she would fling the rock straight at his head. She could hit him, too. Dub had taught her how to chuck a rock straight and true.

"Whitney? What are you doing? Will we eat soon? Is there more water? I'm thirsty."

Mr. Mortalwood's voice had a plaintive note. She looked over her shoulder at him, slumped under a live oak. He seemed shrunken, smaller and more weary than even an hour before. He looked around helplessly, obviously unable to make out the details of his surroundings. Fear trembled in her heart for him, making her momentarily weak.

"We're building you a shelter, Mr. M. Supper's going to take a little while. But there's plenty of water. Have Adrian pass you the jug."

Adrian had elected to tend the fire, the least-strenuous job. He sat, poking at it fitfully with a green stick, tossing pieces of wood on it from time to time. Whitney didn't stop to wonder if he resented her saying he should get water for Mr. M. She couldn't worry incessantly about Adrian's feelings; there was too much else to worry about.

She turned back to her task and hacked so hard that the branch split off from the tree, free, except for one strip of bark.

"Steady, Miss Shane," Gabe counseled. "Not so violent. Trees have feelings, too. Better move on to another. You've wreaked enough havoc on that one."

Taking a deep breath, Whitney said nothing and shifted to a smaller pine. She didn't mind letting him feel the vibrations of her anger, but she wouldn't give him the satisfaction of putting her anger into words. She began to try to wrest off another branch.

"As for what we do next, well, you'd better 'organize your priorities' and 'delegate the responsibilities.' In a situation like this, the first thing to do is tend the injured. We've done that as best we can. The second thing is to find water. We've done that. Next, get food and shelter. We're doing that now. Do you want to cook the mussels while I gather some Spanish moss to sleep on?"

"No," Whitney said with forced politeness. "I *don't* want to cook the mussels. I don't know how. After I see you do it, I will. I'll get the moss."

He laughed. He looked up at the huge live oaks behind them. "Alas, Miss Shane, little of the moss hangs low. You'll have to climb a tree for it."

Whitney's hands were roughened by bark and sticky with sap. She had helped tow a lifeboat today, she'd tracked a raccoon, and she'd slimed herself with mud gathering mussels. Now she seemed to be in hand-to-hand combat with a platoon of pines, and she was in no mood to be trifled with.

"I'm perfectly capable of climbing a tree, Mr. Cantrell. I'll get your moss. Then we eat. Then what?"

He scooped an armful of boughs and started back toward the center of the clearing. He gave her a wry, measuring look, silent laughter in his gray eyes. "Know what, Miss Shane? For an executive, you have surprising talents. You can use a casting net—or so you say. You can track a raccoon—more or less. You're not afraid of snakes or mud, and you can climb trees. Know what? I think, for all your polish, you had a seriously misspent youth as a tomboy."

His words, she knew, were jesting, but they fell like stones on her heart. The bough came loose in her hand, and she stood motionless for a second, numb. *A misspent youth.* That was exactly what she'd had. She never talked about it. She'd never revealed the details to anyone, even Lila Mortalwood.

He, too, paused a moment, watching her face. He said nothing, only studied her with a disconcerting intentness. *He's got eyes like a wolf or a hawk,* she thought. *It's as if he can see right through me.*

Hurriedly she glanced away and concentrated on gathering her scattered heaps of boughs.

"Whitney?" Mr. Mortalwood called from the heart of the clearing. His voice had an unfamiliar quaver in it. "Will we have to sleep here? How will we sleep?"

"Don't worry, Mr. M.," she said, trying to pull her thoughts together. "I'll tend to it. You'll be taken care of."

Gabe had turned from her and headed back toward the other men. She was grateful. Suddenly she realized one of the reasons he disturbed her so profoundly.

Other people always saw her as she was—young, bright, successful, capable.

Gabe Cantrell gave her the uneasy impression he saw the same things. But he could see much more. It was as if he saw deep within her the secret she had hidden so well, the child she had once been. He could look into her eyes and see young Whitney Breux Shane, still frightened, still set apart from the world, still in need.

She bit her lip. It was as bad as if he saw her naked.

CHAPTER SIX

WHEN THE FIRE died down and the stone-lined pit was full of glowing coals, Gabe scraped the embers away and covered the heated rocks with seaweed. He placed the mussels, onions and mushrooms in it. Over everything he put a covering of grass, then a thick sprinkling of earth.

With a sharp stick, he punched a hole down to the seaweed layer, poured in more water, then covered the hole. "Everything should be done in an hour or so," he assured Mortalwood. Mr. M. nodded as if he didn't quite understand. Adrian grumbled at the time it took to cook the meal.

He also grumbled at the indignity of Whitney's climbing in the live oaks. "Vice presidents don't climb trees, Shane," he called up to her. "What are you trying to prove? That your ancestors were monkeys?"

Whitney turned cold at Adrian's gibe at her ancestors. "The alternative," she said, all sweet reason, "is to change places. Want to come up here, Adrian?"

Adrian merely snorted and ignored her. He was trying to weave the pine boughs into the long bare limbs of the lean-to's frames, a job for which he was ill-equipped.

Whitney almost smirked from her perch. The tree, although large, had been easy to climb, for its trunk slanted at a gentle angle and its branches were placed so they were easily scaled.

But Adrian, she thought with a glee that bordered on evil, could never climb it. He had probably never climbed a tree in his life. No wonder the man couldn't handle a pine branch, she thought; he'd spent his life punching buttons and allowing machines to wait on him.

When she was done gathering moss, she and Gabe finished threading the boughs into the shelters and let Adrian sit back on his tree stump, where he drew futile maps on the ground with a stick.

Though she and Gabe avoided talking to each other, she knew the large lean-to was for the men, the small one for her. She distributed the moss accordingly, taking little for herself so that Mr. M. might have the most. She made him lie down until supper was ready, and he did so without protest.

She took a brief break and sat down to explore the contents of her purse, wishing for once in her life that she wasn't so well organized.

Another woman who landed on a deserted island and managed to retain her purse might have found herself armed with any number of unexpectedly wonderful things: a nail file or scissors, medicines, chocolate bars or after-dinner mints, rubber bands, hand lotion, hairpins.

But Whitney's purse contained no such riches. She had a hairbrush, a compact, a tube of lipstick, sunglasses, and her wallet, containing one hundred and fifty dollars in cash and all the better credit cards.

Sitting on a stone, staring at the money and cards, she laughed softly. In Atlanta, if she had been hungry, she would have gone to her favorite restaurant, The Abbey, and there, under its vaulted ceilings, eaten the finest of meals.

Had she been weary and somehow unable to reach her town house, she could have pulled out one of her cards and charged a lovely night's sleep in Atlanta's poshest hotel.

Had she wanted food, clothing or any sort of supply, she could have shopped at a dozen different malls, and her cards would have bought her whatever she wished, from Neiman Marcus or Sak's Fifth Avenue or even Tiffany's.

But here on the island, her money could buy nothing and her credit cards were a joke. She laughed again.

"What's so funny, Shane?" Adrian demanded, giving her a humorless look. "We're stuck in this hellhole and we've got nothing. Nothing."

She looked at the steam rising from the cooking pit, at the water jug, still partly full, and the two lean-to's with their beds of moss. "I don't know, Adrian," she said airily. "We've got the sun in the daytime and the moon at night, or however the song goes. Can't you just pretend you're at camp?"

"Camp?" He almost spat the word in disgust. He turned his fuming gaze from her and began to scratch a new map in the earth.

Whitney screwed up her courage and snapped open her compact. Her face was sun-burnished but not burned. Her lips were dry, so she touched them with lipstick, then brushed out her hair, which was wild, a shoulder-length mass of gold. It was stiff from the sea's salt, but she did the best she could, twisting it into a ponytail she fastened with a thread from her cardigan.

From his stump Adrian muttered, "At least I've got some plans to get us out of here alive."

Whitney's muscles tautened. If Adrian had plans, she suspected they weren't realistic. Gabe was the one who would know what to do. She sensed trouble coming as surely as if the wind had changed, suddenly growing cold, portending storm.

THEIR DINNER, although humble, tasted wonderful to Whitney. "Hunger is the best sauce," her grandmother had always said, and it was true.

Adrian ate ravenously, complaining all the while. He missed salt and pepper, the mussels were tough, the onions too strong, and he suspected the mushrooms might not be safe.

Whitney concentrated on trying to get Mr. Mortalwood to eat. His first few bites were enthusiastic, but once the edge was off his hunger, he lost interest and seemed to lose himself in a world of his own, like a daydreaming child. Whitney urged and cajoled the rest of his meal down him, anxious that he keep his strength up.

Afterward, without protest, he let her put him back to bed on the heaped moss. He closed his eyes immediately, and she couldn't tell if he slept or simply lay in a quiet daze.

Adrian watched them closely. When Whitney returned to sit between him and Gabe, he gave her a cool glance. "Mr. M.'s in no shape to take charge," he said, his voice clipped. "So it's my place."

Gabe stifled a yawn and moved to stir the coals back to life. Whitney, seated on a rock, stiffened, her gaze darting from Adrian to Gabe and back to Adrian.

"Our first priority is to get help," Adrian said. "That means a signal. I want Cantrell to build a series of fires along the shore tonight. To alert any passing plane or boat. With luck, we might be out of here by morning. In the meantime, Whitney, it's imperative we have food and water, so I appoint you to be in charge of those matters. Now would be a good time to refill the water containers. You should also put in a fresh supply of those accursed mussels. Third—"

"Hold it," Gabe said, rising so that he towered over their sitting figures. The late-afternoon light filtered through the trees in a golden haze, making him look like a man cast out of bronze.

Whitney tensed more apprehensively than before.

"First," Gabe growled, "it'll take a lot of work and do damned little good to set signal fires on this side of the island. It's also dangerous."

"Nevertheless—" Adrian began, his voice icy, but Whitney interrupted him.

"Why?" she asked Gabe. "Why is it dangerous?"

"You've seen what the wind's like on that beach," Gabe said. "It never stops. It hasn't rained for five weeks. This whole island is like a tinderbox. One stray spark, and *whoosh.*"

He made a gesture with his hand, describing the sweep of fire across the island.

"Not if you tend them," Adrian retorted. "I'm talking about rescue. And I'm in charge. We'll do as I say."

Whitney rose and faced both men. "Adrian, you've taken the liberty of putting yourself in charge. I don't see the necessity. Our best chance is to cooperate and for each of us to do what we do best. I say that we—"

"I *am* doing what I do best," Adrian almost snarled. "I'm organizing things. I'm making decisions."

"And I say we organize and make decisions together," Whitney stated, crossing her arms. "We also pool our knowledge. Mr. Cantrell said that no boats were likely to pass on this side of the island. As for planes, the only one I saw all day was a jet so high it wouldn't notice a fire clear down here. Building fires and tending them all night would be labor probably spent in vain—plus, we're all exhausted. None of us should try to stay up all night. And the island *is* dry. Fires in that wind *would* be dangerous. I vote with Mr. Cantrell."

"Dammit," Adrian said angrily, his dark eyes snapping, "somebody has to take charge. Somebody has to give orders."

Gabe gave a short laugh and put his fists casually on his hips. But his eyes, fastened on Adrian's lean form, were not amused. "I don't think I'll *take* orders from you, Fisk," he said out of the corner of his mouth.

Whitney sensed the tension rising between the two men, and the warning in Gabe's voice made the hair on the back of her neck prickle. She moved to Adrian's side and put her hand on his bony shoulder.

"Adrian," she said, softly but firmly, "this isn't a board meeting. Gabe knows more about this . . . this kind of situation than we do. I say for the time being we follow his advice. And not squabble. The most important thing we can do—for ourselves and Mr. M.—is keep up our morale."

Adrian ignored her. He drew himself up taller and ran his hand through his spiky hair. "We should also," he said, as if Whitney hadn't spoken, "consider adding variety to our diet, especially if we have to spend any length of time on this island. I suggest that you do some foraging while it's light, Whitney. You can find berries—"

"All the edible berries have been gone for months," Gabe interrupted, his mouth crooking downward. "This is October."

Adrian shot him a malicious glance. "Then grapes. Wild grapes grow everywhere." He looked back at Whitney, his brows lowering in ill temper.

"Grapes are long gone, too," Gabe countered, his teeth set. "Stop ordering the woman around. Did you hear what she just said? We've got to cooperate."

The wind rose, carrying the first hint of the cool of evening. Adrian shuddered, whether from cold or a spasm of pain Whitney couldn't tell. He hugged himself and glowered up at the two of them. "Persimmons," he said with a mixture of triumph and despair. "Persimmons are a winter fruit. I remember that. I *know* that."

"It's too early for persimmons," Gabe answered. "They're still too sour to eat. But I'll forage, all right. But before I do, you listen to me for a change." He nodded at Whitney, indicating he meant the message for her, as well. "We'll get off this island. At worst, we won't be here any longer than Friday."

"Friday?" Whitney gasped, surprised. "How do you know?"

"Friday?" Adrian echoed in horror. "That's three more days—we've got to get off sooner than that!"

"We can hang on until Friday with no problem," Gabe said with confidence.

"Why would we be rescued Friday?" Whitney wanted to know, truly puzzled.

Gabe smiled so that the dimples showed with scornful mirth under his stubble. "The Fredericks estate lets a limited number of campers use this place. On Friday, a group is coming. A troop of Boy Scouts from Savannah."

"Boy Scouts?" Adrian almost shrieked in dismay. "We have to be rescued by Boy Scouts? Of all the absurd, humiliating—"

Whitney bit her lip to keep from smiling. She had a sudden vision of Adrian hobbling onto a rescue boat surrounded by helpful little boys in uniform.

"In the meantime," Gabe said, unfazed, "there're things you should know. Number one, never take a step on this island unless you're watching where your foot goes. There's cactus, there are burrs, there are fire ants, and there are rattlesnakes. Also alligators."

"Alligators?" Adrian cried in horror. "Alligators?"

"Keep your eyes open and you'll be fine," Gabe said dispassionately. "Now, I'm going foraging."

He turned to Whitney, looking her up and down with the same lack of emotion. "You can come or you can stay here.

If you stay, keep the fire exactly that size. I repeat—it's dry here, damned dry. If a fire gets out of hand, it could sweep through these trees faster than they could outrun it." He nodded toward Adrian and at Mr. Mortalwood, who was still curled motionless on the bed of moss. Whitney had covered him with his torn jacket.

"I'm coming with you," she said without hesitation. "Two can forage better than one."

"Fine," he said curtly. "Fisk, you watch the fire, then. And remember what I said."

Adrian looked up at him, fear mingling with resentment on his face. But for once, he said nothing. He kept hugging himself, as if he felt some mysterious chill that touched no one else.

"Come on," Gabe muttered. He stooped to pick up his stained and crumpled shirt. Wordlessly, Whitney took up her ruined cardigan and went with him. This time neither of them tried to take the lead. They walked to the beach side by side, like companions, equals, people who had known and respected each other a long time.

On the beach the wind was higher than before, and the waves hissed and rumbled. Whitney glanced up at Gabe's profile, his mane of bright hair tossing in the breeze.

"What do you want me to do?" she asked matter-of-factly. "I meant what I said. You know more about this than I do."

He stopped, scrutinizing her. In his eyes, curiosity seemed mixed with some strong emotion he held rigidly in rein. "I'm taking the raft out to where the boat sank," he said shortly. "I want you to comb the beach. We went north for the mussels. Scout south. Pick up anything you think we could use. You've got a good eye. I trust you."

His offhand compliment set an odd tremble racing through her midsection. But his words also made her tense with foreboding.

"Clear out there? In the raft? Is that safe? Why?"

He shrugged one bare shoulder. "I'll be careful. I want to see if I can scavenge anything. We're down to bare-bones survival here. If it was just you and I—and even Adrian—I wouldn't worry. We'd do fine. But Mortalwood's another story."

Mr. Mortalwood in danger? Whitney's heart froze. "What do you mean?"

Gabe reached out to take her by the shoulders, as if to reassure her. But he stopped himself, his face hardening, and his hands dropped back to his side. Once more, so close to being touched by him, Whitney was certain her heart had ceased beating.

Gabe pushed his hand through his tossing hair in frustration. "He's an old man. He's not in good health. He's been shaken up, and he doesn't seem to be bouncing back very well."

"You don't think he'll *die?*" Whitney asked in horror. The thought was too terrible to contemplate. Lawrence Mortalwood couldn't die—not so soon after Lila. Lila had been like a surrogate mother to her, and she knew Lila would want her to take care of Mr. M. She couldn't fail. She couldn't.

Gabe watched the naked emotions crossing her face. "No," he said carefully. "I don't think he'll die. But I want to be careful with him. Or it could take him a long time to recover."

"His medicine," Whitney said, suddenly understanding what worried Gabe. "You want to find his medicine. Especially his blood-pressure medicine. Good grief, all of this might have given him a small stroke or something...."

One bronzed brow arched in cynical wonder. "Sometimes you're *too* bright, Miss Shane. But neither of us is a doctor. We can only guess, and in the meantime take as good care of him as possible."

Whitney shook her head in consternation. She didn't want to look into Gabe's measuring eyes any longer, so she stared down at the sand. "We don't even know if there's anything left of the yacht. I thought I heard a second explosion. . . ."

"So did I," he agreed. "But we won't know unless I look. You don't mind scouting the beach by yourself? You're not afraid of that alligator?"

She glanced up, resenting that he would tease her when so many serious matters faced them. "I'm not afraid of alligators," she said impatiently. "It wouldn't be the first time in my life I saw an old alligator."

He shook his head and smiled. "What a woman. What a kid you must have been. Not afraid of snakes or mud *or* 'gators. All the little boys must have loved you."

Her heart, which had seemed so achingly paralyzed, suddenly rapped against her ribs too swiftly for comfort. "No," she said, unable to stop meeting his gaze. "They didn't. Not at all."

Other children, boys and girls alike, had teased her about having no father, had made her an outcast. She had never fit in.

Gabe's eyes were serious as they studied her expression, but his slanted smile stayed in place. "Then they were all very stupid little boys," he said.

The waves rolled like muted thunder, and the sea behind him swayed and glittered. Whitney turned away. "If you can find any regular food for Mr. M. . . ."

"I'll bring anything I can find that'll make him more comfortable," he promised, his voice low, yet oddly harsh.

She was too filled with emotion to speak. She nodded wordlessly and began to pace alone down the deserted beach.

Later, after she had walked a long time, she raised her eyes and looked out to where he had gone, the raft bobbing on the waves like a toy boat. Gabe was a mere speck against the water. Whenever he dived, the speck disappeared beneath the heaving surface, was gone too long, then reappeared just when fear for him began to grip her enough to hurt.

THEY MET AGAIN as the lowering sun was starting to gild the clouds and tint the sky. Gabe came slogging through the waves, pulling the raft. He had put on his shirt, and the sea had washed it nearly clean again. He shook the water from his hair and grinned his crooked grin.

She had her tattered cardigan stuffed with objects she had found along the beach, and under one arm she carried a stack of bleached, flat, bonelike plates, almost rectangular in shape.

"Ah," he said, hauling the raft on shore. "It's show-and-tell time. How'd you do?"

Whitney pushed a fluttering strand of hair from her eyes and tried to sound as businesslike as possible. "The important question is how did you do? You were out there a long time. What did you find?"

"Pull up some seaweed, sit down, and I'll show you," he said, tugging the raft farther out of the water.

Whitney sank onto the sand gratefully. She had walked a long distance, and she was exhausted. She had been fueling herself all afternoon on adrenaline and sheer nerve. She was thirsty, too, which reminded her that she should go to the spring and refill the water containers.

Oh, she thought wearily, brushing her unruly hair from her face, there was so much to do, so much to keep on doing; would she ever feel rested or secure again?

If Gabe was tired, he didn't show it. The muscles in his long arms and legs rippled smoothly as he pulled the raft up in front of her, then sat at her side.

"A blanket," Whitney said, feeling pleased yet a bit dull. A soaked blanket, torn at one corner, lay atop the other objects in the raft. "Good—Mr. Mortalwood can use it. The wind's so high it shouldn't take long to dry, should it?"

"A blanket's the least of our miracles," he said. "And I want to tell you, everything in this raft *is* a miracle. That engine blew apart—a spark must have hit the gas supply." He shook his head. "You should see what's left. Or rather, what isn't." He wasn't smiling now.

"What do you suppose happened?" she asked, alarmed at his sudden somberness.

He shook his head again, shrugged. "Who knows? The marine authorities and the insurance people will have to figure it out. The old tub had been neglected, and something went blooey. Mortalwood can probably sue."

"Sue," Whitney repeated, depressed at the thought of all of this tribulation leading only to litigation.

"But," Gabe went on, as if he sensed her sinking spirits, "somebody up there likes us. I found what counts. I think." He reached under the blanket and pulled out a black leather briefcase, badly scuffed. In its corner was a tastefully carved monogram, LLM.

Whitney's energy surged back in a tide of excitement. "Mr. M.'s briefcase!" she cried. "Did you look? Is his medicine there?"

"It's there," he said, watching her pleasure with apparent satisfaction. "Not even wet. It pays to buy the finest in leather. I'll have to remember that if I'm ever in the market for a briefcase."

Almost grinning with glee, Whitney opened the case. Gabe was right. The bottles of pills and capsules were all there, and even the papers within the briefcase were hardly damp.

The papers, she thought with a frisson of apprehension. The papers were Mr. Mortalwood's notes about buying Sand Dollar Island. Had Gabe seen them? He must have if he'd opened the case. Quickly she snapped it shut again.

She looked at him, searching his face for any indication that he knew what the papers were about. But his expression told her nothing, and he seemed to have other concerns on his mind. He threw the blanket farther back. "And how's this for a miracle?" he asked, handing her four cans of soup. She set down the briefcase and took them.

"Soup," she said joyously, immediately forgetting about the notes about the sale of the island. The soup cans were dented, their labels wet, wrinkled and peeling, but enough was left to tell her what treasures lay inside: three chicken noodle soups and one vegetable.

"This is wonderful," she said, "We'll save it all for Mr. M. He needs it more than anyone else."

"Fine," Gabe agreed tonelessly, "but you ought to think of yourself, too. You're expending more energy than he or Fisk."

"I've got more," she answered. "What else do you have?"

His trove of treasures was mixed, but every item looked wonderful to Whitney: a chair's plastic cushion—she could now see that Mr. M. had a pillow for his head; a large, if badly dented saucepan; a plastic pail; a sodden valise half-full of clothes—Mr. Mortalwood's. There were also several ropes, an assortment of lengths of wire, a plastic coffee mug and a six-pack of ginger ale.

Whitney, too, had found a length of rope and a piece of cord perfect for patching the fishnet. She had scavenged another plastic gallon jug, several more two-liter plastic bottles, a crumpled canvas tote bag and a pint-size glass jar.

Finally, she had found part of the sun- and wind-scoured shell of a giant turtle and taken six of the nearly rectangular stomach plates. They were pointed at one end, and might be used as digging tools. At least they were flat, and if nothing else, could serve as plates.

Proudly she showed Gabe her finds, saving the best for last: a tangled length of nylon fishing line with a weight and large hook still attached. He whistled softly in appreciation. Now they had two ways to catch fish, the net and the hook.

He gave her his off-center smile. It made the laugh lines around his eyes deepen and the long dimples play under the gleaming stubble of his cheeks. She had a sudden and absurd desire to lay the tip of her forefinger against one of those dimples, to feel it working beneath the roughness of his unshaven beard.

"We're a fine pair of scroungers." Grinning lazily, he reached for one of the cans of ginger ale and popped it open. "I say let's drink to us."

He passed her the can for the first sip.

Whitney's brow creased in concern. "We shouldn't. We should save it for Mr. M. And Adrian. I mean, Adrian's being awful, but he *is* hurt, and I don't need anything special—"

"Drink it," he ordered. "We've earned this. Don't say we haven't."

"But I shouldn't even be sitting here," she protested, "We've got the medicine—I should get it back to Mr. M. And I need to get more water for everybody."

He shook his head. "Mortalwood's probably still asleep. He needs rest as much as he needs medicine. You need rest yourself. You're not made of iron, you know. Even if you think so. Drink. You know you're thirsty."

She considered his words and nodded. She *was* thirsty. The windswept, sun-drenched beach had parched her throat.

He watched her turn the can in her hand, examining the label as if it was some foreign object from a world that had disappeared forever.

"Make a toast," he suggested.

She thought for a moment, then smiled. "To the Boy Scouts," she said, raising the can in tribute. "May we get off Sand Dollar before we need them." Then she frowned. "But why didn't you tell me from the beginning about them?"

"I don't know. You'd been kind of uppity. To keep you in suspense maybe. Drink." She took a long sip, reveling in the tangy rush of the soda in her mouth. She passed the can to him. He didn't wipe away her lip prints, simply pressed his mouth against them and drank. Then he handed the can to her.

She stared at it a moment. To show him she wanted no intimate contact with him, she should wipe the can. She should, in fact, make a show of it, just to keep him in his place.

But she couldn't bring herself to do it. Instead, she simply raised the can and drank again, pressing her mouth to the spot where his had been. They took turns drinking, never speaking. When they finished, Whitney had an odd feeling, as if the two of them, sitting on the sand, the wind tossing their hair, had shared some sort of communion.

She tried to shake away the feeling. "That's got to be my last self-indulgence," she said. "Mr. M's the one who needs all the extras."

Gabe looked away from her, toward the west. The sky was turning fiery with the setting sun. "How do you feel about him, about Mortalwood?" he asked abruptly.

She stared out at the sea, gray, endless, growling its eternal growl. "What do you mean?" she asked, picking up a cockleshell. "He's my employer. He's been . . . my mentor. At least his wife certainly was. I'm concerned about him for her sake, as well as his. I like him. I feel . . . grateful."

"Grateful," Gabe said in a tone that radiated irony. "Are you sure? Is that why you're always fussing over him?"

Whitney gave him a sidelong look, but he was still gazing up at the sky, almost as if he'd forgotten she was there. "I fuss over him because he's hurt," she said with spirit. "Of course, I'm fond of him. But don't get any sleazy ideas. He's almost old enough to be my grandfather."

He nodded, but said nothing.

Oh, Whitney thought tiredly, *what's he up to now? Just when I think we might be friends, he always says something to ruin it.*

She rose to go and was surprised when he was on his feet faster than she. He towered over her. He had unbuttoned his shirt and it flapped in the wind, revealing the blue alligator. The sight of it made her uneasy, and she looked away.

She reached for her bundle and the briefcase and tortoise plates, picked them up, then stepped toward the path that led to the camp. But Gabe was suddenly in front of her, blocking her way. She found herself staring at the alligator again. Swallowing, she forced herself to look up into his face instead.

All traces of his smile were gone. He was her stone savage again, and his mood, for some unfathomable reason, seemed to border on the dangerous. "If that's how you feel about him," he said slowly, his eyes holding hers, "what are you going to do if he tries to convince you that you're indispensable to him? Because it could happen. You're playing Florence Nightingale, and he could start imagining that he can't live without you—that he's even in love with you. You have to know that. And . . . maybe you want it."

Whitney's lips parted, but she was so deeply shocked she could say nothing. She liked Mr. Mortalwood, but she had never harbored any romantic thoughts about him, and she certainly didn't fancy herself his nursemaid. She stared at Gabe in true astonishment.

He nodded curtly. "Is that what you want?"

Once more she felt as if her heart slowed, stumbled, then halted completely. She couldn't get her breath. Her voice seemed lodged, choking, in her throat. "That's ridiculous," she managed to say. "Ridiculous."

"No," he said. "It's not. But I don't blame you. He's got a lot of money. Now run along and give him his pills and make him some hot soup and hold his hand. I'll hang out this blanket to dry and get the water."

As abruptly as he'd blocked her way, he stepped aside so that her path was clear.

"Go on," he repeated, his voice soft, yet rasping with satire. "Go to him. Play your angel-baby-darling act to his sugar daddy."

Furious, wounded to the core, Whitney turned away from him and left so swiftly it was almost like fleeing.

Lawrence Mortalwood fall in love with her? She'd never heard anything as ridiculous. Or as insulting. Mr. M. was more than an employer, but he was a friend only—a deeply trusted and loyal friend who now needed her more than he ever had in his life. And she must be loyal to him in turn.

CHAPTER SEVEN

ADRIAN DEMANDED to know what they'd found, sulked when he learned Whitney hadn't brought the ginger ale, then lapsed into glowering silence.

Whitney reluctantly woke Mr. Mortalwood and cajoled him into taking his medications.

"Whitney, you're a miracle worker," he said, wincing as he shifted on his bed of moss. "How long will we be in this godforsaken place? Can he get us off, the Cantrell man?"

He reached for her hand and squeezed it. When she started to draw away, he kept hold, as if he needed the comfort of human touch. She smiled feebly and laced her fingers through his plump ones. "I'm not the miracle worker," she said. "Cantrell found the medicine. And soup and ginger ale. If you stay awake, you can have some ginger ale."

Mr. Mortalwood nodded and winced again. He held her hand more tightly.

She felt self-conscious, recalling what Gabe had said. But Mr. M. was hurt and in need of simple human comfort, that was all. "As for when we get off," she said, "no later than Friday. Some campers are due."

Once more he nodded. "Friday," he murmured. "That's not so terrible. Not so very terrible."

"It might even be sooner," Whitney said, eager to encourage him. "We've got water, food, shelter and your medicine. Cantrell even found a blanket and a change of clothes for you. Just rest and keep your strength up."

"I wish I had my glasses," he complained. "Is this beach nice? Does it look suitable for what we have in mind?"

She hesitated, her hand locked in his. *For what we have in mind.* She remembered the haunting vista of the empty beach, how small and insignificant she had felt. "The beach," she said slowly, "is beautiful. Yes. It's... quite beautiful."

He squinted and rolled his head from side to side, taking in what he could of his crude shelter and the grove of live oaks. The world was turning shadowy, and she didn't know how much he could see.

Dreamily he said, "I'm going to put a special lodge here. On this very spot. I'll have a suite built for myself, with every luxury—water bed, Jacuzzi, wet bar, fireplace. I'll sit in the Jacuzzi with a martini and laugh about all this."

He squeezed her hand again.

"That's a good idea, Mr. M.," Whitney agreed, because she knew it would soothe him. Yet, unexpectedly, her heart twitched in pain at the thought of an ultramodern lodge replacing the ancient live-oaks. The trees reminded her of a tribe of wise old giants, bending and bearded with age.

"I think a lodge would be redundant here," Adrian said from his stump. He slapped at a mosquito. "We'll have hotels up and down the beach. This would be better for the golf course. Convenient to the beach, not too hilly, not too flat. We'll bulldoze these trees and landscape it—pay a top designer to—"

"Bring it up later," Mr. Mortalwood said wearily. "I don't want to consider alternatives now. Whitney, did you say there was ginger ale?" He looked up at her with hopeful, unfocused eyes.

"Yes, yes," she said, trying to cheer him. "Cantrell has it. He should be along any minute. He went for more water."

Mr. Mortalwood groaned slightly. "My lodge will have a *magnificent* restaurant. Five-star, a Cordon Bleu chef, twenty-four-hour room service, a bar stocked with everything—Dom Perignon, the finest Russian vodka—"

"Shh," Adrian hissed. "*He*'s coming."

Gabe appeared at the edge of the grove, his arms full. He looked at the three of them, his face unreadable, but Whitney sensed that for a second a scalding contempt blazed in his eyes when he saw how tightly Mr. Mortalwood held her hand. Embarrassed, remembering Gabe's words on the beach, she quickly looked away. In the distance the sea rumbled and grumbled, an almost ominous sound.

IT WAS DARK. Through the shaggy leaves and mossy veils of the live oaks, Whitney saw that the moonlight was transmuting the clouds to silvery blue.

"No." Gabe's voice snapped with impatience. "I don't need help. I'll do the fishing. Stay here and be Mortalwood's nursemaid."

She stood at the edge of the grove with him, her hands on her hips. The only way to deal with a man this stubborn, she told herself, was to be more stubborn. "Mr. Mortalwood's asleep," she said firmly. "I want to *know* where these fish are. What if some time I *have* to do the fishing? What if a snake bit you tomorrow, and I had to take care of all three of you? I have to know the ins and outs of this place."

She could barely see his face in the darkness. His shorts and the white of his black-and-white shirt took on a ghostly glow in the moonlight. He cocked his hip at an impatient angle. He tried another tack.

"Look," he said, "you're dead on your feet. Rest. Morning's going to come all too early. If you wear yourself out, you're no good to anybody."

She tossed her head. "I'm going. I can last as long as you can, and I'll pull my own weight while we're here. I won't be dependent on *you*."

He swore under his breath. She had a vision of herself obstinately following him, dogging his steps like an unwanted little sister, rejected yet determined not to be left behind.

"Come on," he half snarled, turning his back. "And don't blame me if you step right *on* an alligator. I hope you do."

She stalked after him. "I'm not afraid of—"

He cut her off. "I know. You're not afraid of alligators. Alligators should be afraid of you. You'd make them into executive briefcases."

It was difficult following him, for in the darkness she could barely see what lay in her path. Several times she felt the piercing pain of a jumping cactus attaching itself to her ankle or burrs scratching her feet where the sandals left them bare. She would rather die, though, than slow down or cry out.

He was going away from the beach, deeper into the woods. At last the rough path gave way to a narrow dirt road. She fell into step beside him, "Where are we going? Why is this road here if the island's deserted? How did you know it was here?"

"Questions, questions, questions," he grumbled, and kept walking.

Now she could clearly see the stars and the luminous clouds overhead. Gabe's face was no longer a mysterious shadow. The light silvered his tossing hair, fell on the clean, straight lines of his features. Once again she was reminded of a Viking, his gaze on some far horizon.

"Well?" she asked pointedly, emphasizing that she'd asked him questions, but that he hadn't answered.

He tossed her a casual glance. "We're going to a bridge," he said, as if he begrudged her every word. "The road's kept up because campers come over, and so do scientists sometimes. I've read about it, talked about it."

"Why?" she demanded. "You're not from around here—you said so. Why study this particular island?"

He sighed harshly, a sound of annoyance. "I wanted to know about it, that's all. An island's ecology is fragile. Most of this one's been left intact, especially this side. Nobody's lived on the other side for almost fifty years. So it's an *interesting* island, all right?"

Her tired mind raced. She'd always suspected he was too intelligent for a mere drifter. Why was he so knowledgeable about this isolated island? Could he be some sort of corporate spy? He hardly seemed the type, but in a business deal this large, anything was possible.

"Why? Why interesting to you?" she prodded.

"Because I find the wilderness interesting," he answered sharply. "All right? Now, if you want to fish, fish. We're here. Do you really know how to use this thing?" He nodded dubiously at the net he carried flung over one shoulder.

Whitney looked at the new scene before her and drew in her breath in wonder. The bridge was old and crudely built, but sturdy. Its weathered planks shone pale gray in the moonlight. A splintery wooden railing ran along each side, and thick pilings plunged down into a narrow, softly flowing river.

Dark water purred beneath the bridge, flickering and twinkling between shadowy banks, its surface reflecting the wealth of lights in the sky.

Beyond the bridge, the forest fell away for a few hundred yards. Wild fields, tall with grasses, waved in the moonlight.

But it was the sky that dazzled Whitney. She could look up and see it unobscured. Thousands of stars—no, she amended mentally, millions of stars—gleamed above her. It was as if someone had spilled all the diamonds of India and Africa across the night.

The moon hung low on the horizon, nearly full, a giant pearl among the diamonds. Its light edged the few stray clouds, bordering them with brightness. It was the sort of sky one never saw in a town or city. It was the sort of sky she hadn't seen since she was a child.

"I asked if you could really use this thing," Gabe repeated. His voice was low, soft, but so near it startled her. For one enchanted moment she had forgotten everything, even herself, aware only of the magical light of the sky.

Then she was all too conscious of Gabe at her side. He, too, seemed to be transformed by the night. He was so tall it made her heart pulse like one of the stars twinkling above them. The breeze tousled his hair, and it gleamed like a crown in the moonlight.

His features were so silvered that, had his hair not blown across his forehead, flickering in and out of shadow, he would have almost been statuelike. But there was no stillness in his eyes. They dwelt on her face with an intensity that almost took her breath away.

Oh, my, thought Whitney in pleasant confusion. *He looks like a knight, and the moonlight is his armor. A man like this could do anything. Anything.*

Immediately she admonished herself for such a wild thought. He wasn't a knight. He was a man with a fishnet and a bad attitude. That was all.

He held the net out to her. "Show me," he said in the same low voice.

Still feeling moonstruck, Whitney willed her emotions to behave and her usual practicality to reign. There were four people to feed. The river might be spangled with silver, but what was important was that it contained fish, which meant nourishment.

"I said I could use it," she said stiffly, taking great care so that her hand did not so much as brush his as she took the net.

He had mended the net and attached a long cord to its center. As soon as she touched it, she seemed to step back in time. She had to loop the long cord just so, she remembered, trusting instinct to help her do it right.

She moved to the middle of the bridge. Gabe stayed close by her side, too close for her to be able to block out her awareness of him. She gritted her teeth in concentration.

When she was a child, such a net reminded her of a mesh petticoat. It was round and resembled lacy fretwork, edged at intervals about the bottom with weights like beads. She remembered Dub's teaching her the intricacies of throwing the thing.

In her mind's eye, she could still see him. Casting a net took some strength, but mostly it demanded coordination. She reexamined the coil of the rope, shook out the net, then took one of the beads at its hem between her teeth.

That was the hard part, she knew, but it had to be done just so, so that when the net was thrown it spun out, forming a circle that dropped onto the water. She took a deep breath and threw the net, at the same moment releasing its beaded edge from between her teeth.

"Drat!" she muttered, for she didn't do it right, and the net didn't spread as far as it should have. She let it settle, then pulled it up out of the water. It came up empty.

But she remembered more clearly now. She recoiled the rope and frowned as she took out the net. She trapped a bead between her teeth again and cast once more, this time releasing the weight at the right moment. The net whirled out over the water, billowing perfectly.

She waited for the weights to sink and close, then pulled the rope and hauled it up again. A small silvery fish thrashed in its meshes. "Ha," she said with satisfaction. "Got you."

"My God," Gabe breathed at her side. "I don't believe it."

"I told you," she said with a triumphant grin. *Dub taught me well,* she thought with a sudden rush of gratitude. After all these years, she finally appreciated just *how* well.

Her smile faded, and she was bewildered because tears sprang into her eyes. She was unexpectedly plunged into a wave of homesickness such as she had never felt before. She was not homesick for her mother or for her stepfather's cheerless house. It was the river she missed, and her grandmother and Dub.

She fought the tears back with all her formidable willpower, glancing out at this river so that Gabe couldn't see her eyes. "Well," she said as calmly as she could, "we caught it. Now what do we do?"

"Keep it. Catch more. We'll take them back to camp and smoke them. They'll be ready to eat by morning."

She nodded, biting her lip. Before they'd left for the river, Gabe had lowered the flames of the small fire until it had burned slowly, barely smoldering. He'd also woven a grate of green alder branches. If the fish were cut into strips and laid on the grate over the fire, the smoke would cook them by morning.

To hide the unexpected surge of emotion that had overwhelmed her at remembering Dub, she opened the net, letting Gabe take the small, flopping fish. He put it on a crude stringer. She gathered up the net and threw it again.

She cast until she was exhausted. It was not easy work, and she knew her shoulders would ache in the morning, but she caught six mullet. Gabe said that they were sea fish that preferred shallows and tidal streams, not difficult to catch.

At last she relinquished the net to him, and sat, exhausted, her arms around her knees, watching him cast. He was far stronger than she was, and the level of his coordination was better.

There was a certain beauty in the action of throwing the net, and he had surprising grace for a man so tall. Tired, cooled by the continuous breeze, she leaned against the railing and watched him. He caught eight more fish, then the net began coming up empty.

Still she watched, hypnotized half by fatigue, half by the strangeness of everything. Tonight she was supposed to have been in a luxury lodge on Hilton Head overlooking a private golf course. If she had been hungry, she would have phoned room service, not gone fishing off a moon-drenched bridge.

She rose to stretch and ease the kinks out of her muscles. She walked to the edge of the bridge to stand beside Gabe. She put her hands on the rough railing and looked down into the water where the net spread, then sank.

He hauled it up again. For a moment, Whitney could not believe her eyes. There were no fish in the net, but it seemed momentarily enchanted by phantom, dancing fire. Blue light flickered in it like ghostly fairy lights that swiftly disappeared.

"What . . . ?" she gasped. Perhaps she was more exhausted than she'd realized. Her eyes were playing tricks.

He turned, giving her his one-sided smile. "Never see that before? I'm surprised it took so long to happen."

"What is it?" Whitney breathed, watching him draw up the net to cast it again. She still didn't believe that she had seen its meshes glitter with phosphorescence as if bewitched.

He made a strong cast into the water, waited a moment, then drew the net up once more. Again it sparkled momentarily with silent flashes of pale blue light. "Plankton," he explained. "Tiny sea creatures. They're phosphorescent. We've found a colony. They get in the net and slip through, but for a moment, they dance. Like fox fire or the will-o'-the-wisp. Want to see it again?"

"Please," she said, fascinated. It was as if he were netting tiny galaxies of stars, but they escaped him, fleeing back into the river's mysterious depths. He showed her again and again, for she couldn't get her fill of the sight. It was both eerie and wonderfully beautiful.

But at last, the plankton, like the mullet, seemed to go. He folded up the net and turned to her.

"You asked me a lot of questions when we first got here," he said, looking down at her.

She felt her stomach do an odd little cartwheel and looked away. She stared up at the sky, almost losing herself in it. Its hugeness, its myriad stars, made her almost dizzy. "Yes?"

"How about I ask you a few?"

The dizziness spun away, replaced by wariness. It was coming, she thought. He was starting to pry again, asking what they were doing on the island. He must have seen Mr. Mortalwood's papers. He must have. Why else would he be so curious? Did he pose some sort of danger to their plans she didn't understand?

She let her eyes meet his again, trying to keep her gaze cool, level and controlled. "You can ask. I may not answer."

He shrugged. He still wore his shirt unbuttoned, and it flapped lazily in the steady breeze. But his question surprised her. "I know who you are," he said, unsmiling. "But who *were* you? Who'd you used to be, Shane?"

She blinked, taken aback. "What?" She pushed an unruly strand of hair back from her face.

He leaned nearer, his eyes narrowing. "You're a high-muck-a-muck in Mortalwood's company. A corporate princess. But you weren't born to it. You worked your way there. From what? Where did you start from?"

She stared up at him, not understanding why he'd asked her this. She didn't want to talk about it. She never talked about it. The past was gone, over. She'd escaped it forever.

"Of course, I worked," she said evasively. "The only way to get anywhere is to work."

"Where'd you come from?" he persisted. "You don't sound like Atlanta. You don't sound like anyplace. You sound like speech class."

"Mississippi," she said shortly. "Southern Mississippi. I didn't *want* an accent. It can hold you back."

He leaned back against the railing and stared up at the starry sky. "We might be here till Friday," he said, abruptly changing the subject. "We may not be able to attract anybody's attention before that."

"I know that." She shifted uncomfortably.

"We're going to get tired of mussels and mullets. I can try to catch other things. A possum maybe. Crayfish. Squirrels. Are you squeamish about eating things like that?"

"No," she said matter-of-factly. "But the others might be. I don't think Adrian or Mr. M. could choke down possum. It's greasy. And you need sweet potatoes or something like that to make it taste decent. Crayfish, the same thing. They might eat them in a sauce, but not without. A squirrel, maybe. A squirrel's not bad. Stringy, a little gamy, but not too bad.''

He turned and looked down at her, his eyes narrowing again. She realized she had just made a mistake, a serious one.

"You've eaten all those things,'' he said, his voice low. "Haven't you?''

She shrugged. Where she had grown up, possum and squirrel and crayfish were poor people's food. She had eaten them, all right.

"Who taught you to fish?'' he asked, bending nearer. "Your father?''

She turned from him, wanting to end the discussion. "No,'' she said shortly. Why did he care, she wondered fretfully. Why did he want to know?

"Then who taught you all this?'' he demanded. "They aren't exactly your typical executive skills, you know.''

"Who taught *you?*'' she countered. "Or did you spend five hundred years in the Boy Scouts?''

She didn't expect it, but he smiled. "You might say it's a specialty of mine—survival living. I told you once—if it were just you and I on this island, I wouldn't worry. I could take care of you fine.''

Whitney bristled. "I can take care of myself fine, thanks.''

He laughed softly. She could feel his eyes on her, hear the flapping of his shirt. She could imagine his wicked smile, white and spellbinding in the moonlight.

"Oh, you're good, Shane, surprisingly good,'' he said. "But I'm better, and you know it. Survival-wise, for somebody healthy, this island's a piece of cake. But I could take care of you anywhere. The Arctic. The desert. The sea. The jungle.''

"Sure of yourself, aren't you?" she asked in a tone that she hoped showed she was unimpressed. "But I don't imagine it's a skill that's in great demand—being able to live like a savage."

He laughed again. The sound made the back of her neck prickle, her midsection tighten.

"I'm not a savage," he said softly. "If I were, you'd know. So would the others. No, I'm civilized. More's the pity."

"Civilized," Whitney gibed, keeping her back to him. She closed her eyes and took a deep breath. The scent of the night wind was so clean, so healing, that she thought if she could just stay there, her thoughts would stop spinning and she could think logically, normally again.

"A savage wouldn't bother with Mortalwood," he said. "He's useless. Worse than useless."

He had moved so close that she could feel the warmth of his lean body, feel his breath tickling her ear. "And a savage would have knocked Adrian Fisk into place long before now—as he so richly deserves. Not I. I'm as polite to him as I can stand to be."

"Which isn't very polite," Whitney said, keeping her eyes shut. She wished he would go away, far away, to the other side of the island. Somehow, he made her feel dizzy, the way the stars did.

"As for you, Miss Shane," he whispered in her ear, his breath stirring her hair and teasing her throat with its soft heat, "as for you, if I were a savage, I'd simply take you. Hold the others back and say, 'She's mine.'"

Alarmed and angry, she whirled to face him, her eyes opening widely. "*Take* me?" she cried in protest. "Say I'm *yours?* That's . . . oafish. If you try to force me to do anything, I'll have the law on you so fast when we get back to the mainland your head will spin. I . . ."

He raised his finger to his lips, a gesture for her to be quiet. "I'd never force you to do anything, dear Miss Shane. I am, as I said, civilized."

He stood too near to her, but she refused to back away. She stared up at him and at the span of stars behind him. All those stars did make her senses whirl, she thought in confusion.

"Stop calling me 'Miss Shane,'" she ordered. "You just do it to be sarcastic—*Mr.* Cantrell."

He reached out and smoothed a strand of her hair. She had told him before never to touch her again, but she did not protest. She did not know why. His hand lingered on her face, and his touch made her feel as if her chest were full of stars, pointed and burning and spinning in the darkness.

"Then don't call me 'Mr. Cantrell.' My name is Gabe. Gabriel. Would you say it?"

The hand stroking her cheek was soothing and exciting at the same time. She felt at once both hot and cold.

"Say it?" he asked again softly, leaning nearer to her still.

Her lips parted. He was going to kiss her, she knew. And she was going to let him. It was madness, but she was drunk on stars and moonlight, and she wanted it.

"Whitney?" he whispered. "Say it. Please."

"Gabriel," she said, barely audibly. "Like the angel."

"No," he answered, shaking his head and bending closer. "No angel. Just a man. Who takes nothing by force. But who'll take—if it's given."

He lowered his mouth to hers. His hands moved to frame her face. And if he had indeed proved to be an angel and wrapped great wings around her, folding her against him, she would not have been surprised.

She felt as if he were about to fly her up into the heart of the swirling stars. She wrapped her arms around his neck, willing to let him take her there.

CHAPTER EIGHT

WHITNEY STRETCHED UPWARD, savoring the overwhelming intoxication of his kiss, the warmth of his hands against her breeze-cooled face.

Her usual world was one of logic, finance, efficiency, careful calculation and unending discipline. Now, that self seemed to fall away like a shell or husk she'd outgrown.

Gabe's touch, the hot, hard, questing pressure of his lips against hers, turned the world to a place wholly and magically sensual.

His mouth upon hers was mobile and exciting, for he knew how to give pleasure as thoroughly as he knew how to take it. His chest, half-bared by the open shirt, pressed against her soft breasts, making them tingle and sweetly ache.

The night wind stirred both Gabe and Whitney's clothing, tossed and mingled their hair. In the distance, the unending pound and purr of the waves echoed, and the clean scent of the sea on the breeze coupled with the wild autumn fragrance emanating from the woods and the fields.

Gabe's hands moved sensuously from Whitney's face to her throat, feeling how strongly her pulses throbbed beneath his touch. His fingers, scarred and callused against the silken arch of her throat, explored the tenderness of her flesh with slow and maddening gentleness.

Then, with dizzying abruptness, his hands fell to her shoulders, pulling her closer to him, more deeply into his kiss. The harsh, unshaven feel of his jaw burned against her softer skin, but she didn't mind. His strength and passion made blue lights dance across the darkness of her mind, like the phantom lights that had danced in the net.

With one arm he caught her tightly around the waist, drawing her more intimately against his long body, and with his free hand, he loosened her hair from what was left of its fastening, running his fingers through its tossing waves.

Whitney gasped in both pleasure and bewilderment. His tongue ran smoothly over her lips, as if to soothe her, then entered between them, as if to show her there was nothing to fear, that the closer they became, the more pleasure they'd experience.

Shyly she tasted him back, and an even greater thrill of delight struck her through. How different their bodies were, she thought hazily, how opposite; his lines were hard and lean where hers were curved and soft, the texture of his face and chest was rough with hair while she was smooth and delicate.

It was as if each of them were half of a whole that yearned and struggled to become one again, to be complete. She gasped again at the power and mystery of it, and this time the sound she made resembled a sob.

He drew back abruptly, his face hovering a few inches above hers. "Maybe you're right," he whispered, his breath labored. His chest rose and fell against hers more swiftly than the rhythm of the crashing of the surf. "Maybe there *is* too much savage left in me. Because right now I'd like to take you, right here, on the boards of this bridge in the moonlight, make love to you until the tide runs out, turns and comes in again."

Whitney opened her eyes and stared at him, dazed by the emotions she had allowed herself to feel. She said nothing because her mind whirled in confusion—she simply did not know what to say.

At her hesitation, Gabe's face grew harsh. "But that wouldn't do, would it?" he asked, his hands moving slowly over her to take her by the shoulders again. "Conditions are a little too primitive, aren't they? You don't want to go home with the chance of carrying an illegitimate little Cantrell, do you?"

He paused and took a deep breath. The set of his mouth grew ironically bitter. "So you must be taunting me. Teasing the hired help again. That's dangerous, Whitney. Be careful."

She blinked up at him in shock. The word "illegitimate" went through her like a spear of cold, driving all warmth from her body. He was accusing *her* of toying with the explosive emotions that sparked between them? In a chilling tide, anger rose within her. She had let him kiss her, that was true. Stupid, but true.

But a kiss was not an invitation to make love, and his presumption galled her. "Listen—" she hissed, almost shaking with the tumult of her feelings.

"No," he commanded, gripping her shoulders more tightly. "There's a little savage in all of us. Even you."

"I'm not..." she protested, trying to shake herself free from his grasp. "I don't...I wouldn't..." But he held her tightly until pride and fatigue finally stopped her from struggling. She was too tired to fight. Let him say what he wanted, then she'd escape.

That's why I didn't fight him before, she thought in weary perplexity. *I was too tired. I was crazy with tiredness.*

She managed one last ineffectual thrust against his chest, but he remained immovable, gripping her, bending over her. "Stop," she said coldly, willing her body to be completely rigid.

Yet her thoughts were in chaos. It had been so wonderful after such a long and grueling day to lean on someone for once, instead of always, endlessly giving strength away.

And she admitted—although it pained her—that it had also been wonderful not to feel alone. All her life since she had left Dub and her grandmother and the river, she had felt alone. It was simply a loneliness that had haunted her, bone deep, for years. Tonight in Gabe's arms, it had disappeared. No, she corrected herself. She had *thought* it had disappeared, that was all. She was as alone as ever.

"I don't understand you," he said. His eyes and the line of his mouth looked grim in the moonlight. "But I understand one thing. You weren't meant to belong to an old man. Don't let guilt or loyalty make you throw your life away."

Whitney glared. "I don't know what you're talking about. Let go of me. I'm exhausted. I want to go to bed— alone."

"I'm talking about Mortalwood," he said from between gritted teeth. "Listen to me."

"Oh, stop being ridiculous," she said, turning her face from his.

But suddenly his hand touched her jaw again, making her pulses jump and her chest tighten. Gently but firmly he turned her face so that she had to look at him again. His hand lingered, cupping her chin, and he gazed down at her—but this time there was no laughter in his eyes.

"Whitney..." he said, shaking his head. There was something akin to pain or resignation in his voice.

He bent nearer, and she feared he was going to kiss her again. Worse, she actually *wanted* him to, even now. Was this what her mother had felt on some starry night all those year ago? Wasn't this what Whitney had always been warned against?

This time when she pulled away, he didn't protest. She turned and walked away from him as swiftly as possible. "Bring the fish and the net," she said in her most business-as-usual voice. She made it sound like an order, and she didn't bother to look back at him.

She left him standing on the bridge and hurried back to the safety of the camp and the familiarity of the sort of men she understood.

Adrian was snoring fitfully, but Mr. Mortalwood was awake, lying at the shelter's edge, clutching the blanket to him. It was wrinkled and stiff with salt, but dry.

"Whitney?" he asked when she bent above him. "I thought you'd never get back. I ache all over. Would you get me some water and another sleeping pill? Maybe I could sleep."

Whitney bit her lip. She felt his brow again. His temperature seemed normal, but she couldn't be sure. "I don't know, Mr. M.," she said softly. "I'm not sure you should take another tranquillizer..."

"Whitney, please," he said almost petulantly. "It's terrible not to be able to sleep. It's the loneliest thing in the world—I know. Lila understood. Sometimes she'd fall asleep holding my hand, so it wouldn't be so...bad for me. Please, Whitney."

Her hair was still blowing about her face because she hadn't refastened it. She pushed the fluttering strands back from her face in frustration, not knowing what to do. She didn't want Mr. M. growing too dependent on sedation, but if he lay awake all night in pain, it might sap his remaining strength.

Reluctantly she decided to give in, and she brought him another pill along with a cup filled with water. "Maybe we can find a more comfortable place tomorrow," she consoled him, raising his head so that he could drink.

He choked a little on the pill, alarming her, but he got it down.

"Good night, Mr. M.," she said. "And don't worry. We have plenty of food for breakfast." She patted his hand and went to her own shelter, where she stretched out on the moss gratefully. She was so tired, she thought groggily, she could have slept on stones.

But where was Gabe and why was he taking so long? she wondered, irritated at his absence. Perhaps he would have known what to do about the sleeping pills. Perhaps he could have made Mr. Mortalwood more comfortable.

Whitney burrowed more deeply into the moss. Who needed Gabe Cantrell? she asked herself contrarily. She didn't. She was glad he was gone. She didn't want to think of him or of anything else. All she wanted was sleep.

"Whitney?" Mr. Mortalwood's voice, plaintive, demanded her attention. "Whitney?"

She rose wearily on one elbow, her head spinning with fatigue.

"Whitney, I still can't sleep. Would you stay by me until I do? I . . . I find it a little . . . frightening, all this . . ."

Oh, heavens, Whitney thought, sitting up and briefly burying her face in her hands. He sounded like a sick child in the night, begging for comfort.

Calling on her last resources of strength, she rose and went to him. Once more she settled beside him. The forest creaked and rustled around them and the insects sang. "Don't worry, Mr. M.," she said, trying to sound confident. "You're fine. I'm right here."

He nodded and then settled back into his makeshift bed. He was silent and so was she. She almost drowsed sitting up she was so tired. Somewhere an owl called, an eerie sound, one she hadn't heard in years.

"Whitney?" Mr. Mortalwood's voice quavered, sounding more uncertain than before.

"Yes?" She was startled into wakefulness again.

"What was that noise? Would you—" he hesitated a moment "—hold my hand...until I can get to sleep?"

He's missing Lila, Whitney thought with a wrench of her heart. She missed Lila, too. Nothing seemed to have gone right since Lila's death, and now here they were in this terrible mess....

"Of course, Mr. M.," Whitney said automatically. She took up his hand, patted it and held it loosely in her own.

He sighed painfully. "Thank you..."

She barely heard him. She merely sat beside him, dutifully holding his hand while he struggled to find the oblivion of sleep.

That was how Gabe found her when he finally appeared at the camp's edge.

He stood in the moonlight, staring at her huddled beside Mr. Mortalwood's form, holding the older man's hand in hers. Gabe said nothing. Neither did she. They both looked away.

He must have stayed behind to clean the fish, because now he placed the green wooden grate over the smoky fire and put the silvery pieces on it. Then he rose and disappeared again in the direction of the path.

Where he went, she did not know. She only knew when Mr. Mortalwood finally slept soundly that she was grateful to slip back to her own shelter and lose herself in sleep.

When she awoke the next morning, someone had covered her with Mr. M.'s torn jacket and strewn the moss she slept on with pungent smelling weeds. She recognized the weeds. They were dog fennel, a plant Dub always claimed kept insects away.

Someone during the night had seen to her comfort, and that someone could only have been Gabe. But when she looked across the misty clearing, he was gone again, vanished like a phantom.

"I DON'T NEED any help," Gabe nearly growled. "You'll slow me down. Stay here."

He had returned to camp when the sun was up, not saying where he'd been or why. But Whitney could tell he'd been scavenging. He'd carried the canvas bag she'd found, and it was filled with whelks and mussels. Under his other arm was a bundle of objects he must have found washed up on the shore, mostly ropes and cords and another fragment of net.

She'd already gone for water and seen that Adrian and Mr. Mortalwood ate their share of the smoked fish for breakfast. Mr. Mortalwood could stand this morning and had even walked a little with her assistance.

Gabe had heated the rocks in the steam pit again and buried the mussels to steam for lunch. Now he was ready to explore the other half of the island, and he adamantly didn't want Whitney's company.

"Mr. Mortalwood wants me to go," she said with defiance. "He wants me to see as much as I can. Adrian can hold down the fort here. I'm going."

Gabe tossed a contemptuous glance at Adrian and Mr. M. Adrian had dark circles under his eyes and, when he looked at Gabe or Whitney, malice in his glance. His black hair stood up all over his head and he needed a shave.

He was helping Mr. Mortalwood struggle into a different shirt, one from the valise Gabe had salvaged. Mr. M. was stronger this morning, but Whitney still worried about him. His left leg and arm seemed weak, and she imagined that the left side of his mouth pulled down. His round jaw was bristly with white whiskers, and without his glasses, he squinted in confusion at the world.

Gabe's eyes flicked to her. She'd made herself as presentable as possible, washing at the spring, brushing her hair and braiding it. She'd tied it into two pigtails that she fastened tightly with the yarn from her sweater.

Mr. M. had insisted she take one of his shirts, a pink, long-sleeved one. It was so baggy on her that she had to knot it at her midriff and roll the sleeves to her elbows. She'd put on a good coating of lipstick to protect her lips from the sun and wind. She was rested and ready to go.

Whitney stared at Gabe in cool challenge. Adrian had helped himself to one of Mr. M.'s unworn shirts, but Gabe seemed content with his white shorts and black-and-white shirt. The clothes looked a bit tattered but remarkably clean. She expected he'd already taken a morning swim.

His hair, tousled over his forehead by the breeze, gleamed in the morning light, and the stubble on his jaw shone a darker gold. It was longer this morning, and in another day or two would begin to qualify as a beard.

His eyes, as usual, were narrowed, and he regarded her with an expression of coldness mixed with disdain. "Mr. M. wants it," he said, mocking her words. "Well, certainly— whatever Mr. M. wants. But I'm not slowing down for you or anyone else. Don't blame me if you can't keep up."

Whitney lifted her chin stubbornly. She kept her voice low, so that the conversation remained private. "I've kept up with you so far," she pointed out. It was almost true. She *had* kept up with him remarkably well. She had the aches in her muscles and the scratches on her feet and the scrapes on her hands to prove it.

One of his brows rose in derision and he gave her a cynical smile. "Really? There's an area—or two—where I'm willing and able to go farther than you. A lot farther."

The wickedness in his tone left her with little doubt as to his meaning. He had the insolence to bring up sex. The crooked, self-satisfied smile stayed on his lips, but he looked down at her as if she were some insignificant object a hundred miles beneath him.

Rebelliously she jerked her chin a fraction of an inch higher. "Do you want to stand around talking, or do you want to get something done?"

He laughed, a low, unpleasant sound. "By all means, let's get something done."

He turned toward the overgrown path they had taken last night to the bridge. All he carried was a makeshift canteen, a plastic bottle slung by a cord over his shoulder and the fishing net. She clenched her fists in resolution and followed, determined to keep up.

By the time they reached the bridge, neither of them had spoken. The sight of the bridge, looking even cruder and more weather-battered in the sunlight, seemed to solidify the silence between them. Whitney kept her head down, watching the ground so that she wouldn't have to look at Gabe. He, in turn, made sure his gaze was rarely cast in her direction.

The morning already throbbed with heat, and the sun beat down on them oppressively as they walked through the field beyond the bridge. Whitney silently rejoiced when the road once again led into the thin shade of a scrubby forest. The scent of pine lay heavily on the air.

Once in a while Gabe stopped short, knelt and stared at a set of tracks in the dust, scrutinizing them as if they told a long and complex story. Whitney watched him, frowning as she struggled to remember. Were the blurred prints those of a mouse? A shrew? Or a lizard?

She refused to ask, and he said nothing. He only rose and strode down the road again, making no allowance for her shorter legs. She hurried to keep up, stubbornly maintaining her position at his side and not behind him.

From time to time she was forced to stop because of the insidious jumping cactus that hid in the weeds choking the road. She was surprised that Gabe waited for her the third time she stopped to pull out the spines.

She was even more surprised when he spoke. "Be more careful," he warned her, nodding at the road. "You've got to take care of your feet."

"I know," she answered curtly, but in truth, she was grateful for his concern. The silent hostility between them wore on her worse than the heat. "This stuff," she said, hate for the cactus tightening her voice, "is treacherous, that's all."

Hobbling slightly, she caught up with him. This time when he started walking, he kept his pace slower. The road threaded through another grove of live oaks. Their shade was bliss to Whitney.

"I wish Mortalwood had some extra socks in the valise," Gabe said, looking up at the overhanging branches.

"So do I," she said, her tone heartfelt. Unfortunately Mr. Mortalwood must have unpacked his socks before the yacht sank. She stared down at her scratched ankles. A trickle of blood dribbled down one.

"I'd make Mortalwood give you his," Gabe said, still scanning the live oaks around them. "But I've got his shoes. He needs some sort of protection. And I knew better than to ask for Fisk's."

Whitney shrugged. It had never occurred to her to ask Adrian for his socks, even though she had far more walking to do than he and her feet were far less protected.

"He should have offered them," Gabe observed. "I'll try to get them for you."

"I don't want them," Whitney replied quickly.

Adrian was jealous of his comforts, and she knew he already resented her. She was in better physical shape than he and more knowledgeable in the means of survival. So was Gabe. It seemed to make Adrian seethe.

Besides, Adrian could see that in this crisis Mr. Mortalwood had instinctively turned to Whitney for guidance and comfort. She could tell that Adrian had badly wanted her out of the camp this morning so that he could prove that he was also indispensable to Mr. M.

Gabe gave her a brief sideways glance. "Fisk doesn't wish you well," he said. "He's jealous."

She sighed as the shade fell away and the road bisected another field open to the sun. "Adrian's at a disadvantage," she rationalized. "He hates being dependent. He probably thinks it makes him look bad. He's very conscious of his image."

Gabe stared ahead into the distance and smiled as if to himself. "And he hates competing with a woman. What's the prize? For what are you competing?"

She licked her lips and ran the back of her hand across her forehead, which was dewed with perspiration. "Somebody's going to be appointed executive vice president," she admitted, tired of always evading the truth with him. "We've both worked hard. It makes no difference that I'm a woman."

He halted, and she stopped beside him, puzzled. Once more he laughed his short, humorless laugh. His narrowed gray eyes studied her with cynicism. "Good Lord, you don't believe that, do you?" he asked.

She didn't understand. Her temples throbbed and she wished the sun wouldn't beat down so hard. The sky was such a bright, sharp blue it hurt her eyes. "Believe what?"

"That it makes no difference you're a woman?"

He smiled his one-cornered smile, crossed his arms on his chest. He wore his shirt unbuttoned as usual, giving her yet another disconcerting glimpse of the blue alligator. Suddenly she recalled the incident on the boat when she had been thrown against him and when for a moment her lips had pressed against that very spot above his heart, against the harsh crispness of his golden hair. Her mouth tingled.

Unsettled, she looked across the waving grasses of the field. Their green was turning yellow in the long, autumn dry spell. She took a deep breath, unconsciously rubbing at her lips with her fingertips. "I've never asked for special treatment from anybody because I'm a woman. I've worked as hard as any man. Harder than most. I can compete on equal terms."

He laughed. "That's probably what scares him. And if his chance comes, he'll knife you in the back on equal terms—just as if you were a man."

Whitney pushed back an errant strand of her blond hair. "He might. I'll just have to watch my back, won't I? Come on. Let's get out of this sun."

She started down the road again, glad that another stand of pines was in sight to give them shade. He stayed at her side, easily keeping pace with her.

"Maybe it's too late," he observed laconically. "Maybe he's already stabbed you in the back."

She glanced at him in surprise. *Blast it, he's maddening,* she thought helplessly. *He's been too smart all along, he sees too much, he guesses too well, but what's he mean this time?*

"What I mean," he said as if reading her mind, "is that the three of you want this island. That is, Mortalwood's company wants it, and you three are the heart of the company. But if it's for sale, nobody else knows about it. Unless there's already been some wheeling and dealing. A lot. There has, hasn't there? And Fisk has done most of it."

Her throat went drier than before. The hot breeze slapped at her cheeks, burning them. Her heart began to hammer insanely in her chest. Were they that transparent, she and Mr. M. and Adrian? Gabe had guessed exactly what they were doing. Or had he read more of Mr. Mortalwood's papers than she'd expected?

"I . . ." she said, stammering slightly, "I'm not at liberty to discuss this. I can't say . . . anything."

Suddenly they were in the shade again, for which she was infinitely grateful. Her head ached and her throat burned with thirst and her ankle hurt where the last cactus had pierced her.

Her eyes had trouble adjusting to the shadows. The sun still seemed to penetrate her eyes. She felt a razor-sharp pain in the other ankle and looked down in dismay. Another of the accursed jumping cacti had attached itself to her skin.

"Sit," Gabe unexpectedly commanded. His hand, lean and firm, was on her shoulder, steering her toward a large, lichen-covered stone that lay in the shade of the tallest pine.

"Sit," he repeated, and without protest she did so, grateful that he knelt and took the cactus from her ankle with his work-hardened fingers, sparing her the task. A bright drop of blood welled from the new puncture.

"You've got to watch where you step," he muttered sternly. "And you need water. Why didn't you ask for it? My God, you're the stubbornest woman I ever saw. An island environment like this is tricky. Drink whenever you're thirsty. I mean it."

He thrust the bottle at Whitney and she opened it, taking two small and economical swallows. She tried to hand the bottle back to him so that he, too, could take the edge from his thirst. He refused, pushing it back into her hand.

He still knelt at her feet, her ankle hot and throbbing in his other hand. "Drink," he ordered.

"I can't," she said. "This is only a two-liter bottle. If we don't find water, it has to last us all the way back to camp."

"*You* have to last all the way back. Don't worry about water. Trust me."

She drank again. The water tasted like the nectar of the gods as it slid down her throat. She closed her eyes and savored it. This time when she handed him the bottle he took it.

But instead of drinking, he tore a square the size of a handkerchief from the tail of his shirt and soaked it with water until it was drenched.

"Don't!" Whitney cried, alarmed. "You're wasting it. And your shirt..." He ignored her. He scrubbed the scratches and punctures on both her ankles, then rinsed the cloth again and wiped them once more.

The water felt divinely cool against her burning ankles, but she couldn't believe he was indulging in such a wanton waste of water. It was so unlike him.

"What if we don't find any more?" she demanded. "What are you doing?"

He had taken off his shirt. His golden shoulders gleamed in the dappled light, and she watched the movement of the muscles in his arms and back. Methodically he began ripping the shirt into long strips.

He tugged off her sandals and began to bind the foot that had the most scratches. "Don't worry about water," he said between his teeth. "We'll find plenty. Didn't you see the tracks? Stopped watching, didn't you? That's how the cactus got you."

Tracks? she thought in confusion. Of course. He meant animal tracks. If he'd seen many, it could be a sign of water. And he was right. She hadn't been watching. His questions and his remark about Adrian's stabbing her in the back had diverted her attention, making her careless.

Numbly she watched him as he bound first her left foot, then her right halfway to the knee. "There," he said with satisfaction. He gave her calf a friendly squeeze. "That ought to take care of you for a while."

"Your shirt," she said unhappily, watching him fold the little that was left, no better than a few rags, before stuffing it into his pocket.

He grinned his lopsided grin, gave her calf another comradely squeeze, then slid her sandals back onto her feet. He stood.

"Your shirt," she repeated, shaking her head.

"You need it worse than I do," he said. "You've got to learn to watch where you step. You're too easily distracted. Train yourself. You've got the discipline."

She looked down at her feet, as neatly bandaged as if she wore some sort of jester's tight hosiery, a motley mix of black and white. She looked up at him again, standing barechested, his mane of hair bright against the darkness of the pines.

"We're almost there," he said, nodding back toward the road. "Are you ready to go on?"

He reached his hand out to help her from the stone, but Whitney ignored it. Standing there, bronzed and half-naked, he reminded her again of some sort of handsome, primitive sun god. It seemed wiser not to touch him. He might burn her. Perhaps it was wiser not even to look at him. He might blind her.

She rose and moved toward the road, carefully watching each step she took. "Thank you," she said softly, sensing him fall into step beside her.

"It's not far," he said, ignoring her thanks. "To the Fredericks estate. Or what's left of it. Just beyond this stand of pine. Over that rise."

Whitney nodded, keeping her eyes on the road. She saw one of the low-lying, traitorous little cacti and stepped aside to avoid it. The motion brought her closer to Gabe, making her brush his bare arm. She quickly stepped away from him again, her flesh tickling where she'd touched him.

In silence they climbed the slight rise. From the trees a fish crow called harshly and another answered.

Gabe stopped. Biting her lip, still staring down, she stopped, as well. The silence pulsed between them for the space of a second.

"We made it," he said. "We're here."

Slowly she raised her eyes. Directly before her was another stand of live oaks, widely spaced, draped with gray moss. Occasional scrub pines and other bush grew between them, but the oaks' shade had blocked out most ground growth.

Here and there was stone rubble, the remains of buildings burned and fallen forty years ago. And, at the far edge of the grove, stood three weathered gray walls of rough stone. Beneath them was a fair-sized floor of flat fieldstone, with tufts of grass growing between the cracks.

Even a sagging portion of roof remained. Light shone through the broken shingles but, Whitney thought with delight, the roof could easily be patched, at least temporarily. It must have once been some sort of storage house.

A few yards beyond the walls, ferns and palmettos grew, and something twinkled among them. A stream, Whitney thought with a rush of joy. A tiny, flowing brook. Everything would be easier here: stronger shelter, more water, water right next to them.

Best of all, just beyond the live oaks she glimpsed an orderly group of short, twisted trees. Here and there jewels of bright red seemed to flash from their shadowy leaves. An apple orchard—fresh fruit! Hope swelled wildly in her breast.

"Well?" Gabe said beside her. She looked up at him, and he was smiling. It wasn't his usual crooked smile. It was a gentle one. "Was it worth the trip?"

Whitney drew in her breath with pleasure, her mind racing. She was so happy she could have hugged Gabe, thrown her arms around his waist and pressed herself against his chest. But she dared not do that. No, instead, she had to think.

The wind was milder on this side of the island, and it was nearer the usual routes that boats took. Gabe had said so; they were much closer to possible rescue here. And who knew what treasures might lie among the ruins, treasures that might aid in their survival, make things easier until rescue came?

She calculated the pluses as fast as she could. If there were apple trees, there might be other trees that bore fruit and edible nuts, as well; and water and fruit would attract game—she knew a thing or two about snaring game, and that meant Gabe knew a hundred things. If it was there, he could catch it—and they would have meat.

"Well?" Gabe repeated, waiting for her reaction.

"It's wonderful," she said, smiling widely. "I can't wait to get Mr. Mortalwood here. He'll be so much better off. I'll feel so much safer about him. You don't know how I've worried."

Her eyes met his with what she hoped was a look of gratitude. But his gaze had suddenly gone cold. The smile that had touched his lips died.

"Of course," he said dryly, his mouth twisting. "Your precious Mr. Mortalwood. The goose who lays your golden eggs. Has he proposed yet? I don't imagine he can resist you much longer. Do you really think he'll make you happy? Or is that all that *can* make you happy—money and power?''

CHAPTER NINE

WHITNEY'S BRIEF MOMENT of happiness vanished. Outrage was all she felt. But she wouldn't dignify Gabe's accusations with an answer. Her face went blank as stone.

She turned from him and squared her shoulders. If that, perversely, was how Gabe insisted on seeing her—and her relationship to Lawrence Mortalwood—let him, she thought with cold rancor.

Let him think whatever he wished. She marched toward the orchard, refusing to acknowledge him by so much as a backward glance.

The scent of apples stirred in her a nostalgia she didn't want to acknowledge. It was a sweet, ripe, haunting, autumn scent, the sort that makes a person drunk with memories. She tried to shake away old and useless recollections and concentrate on the work at hand.

Methodically she began gathering apples. There was a wealth of them and, to her delight, occasionally a perfect one, which she put aside. The others, bruised or wormy but with edible parts, she placed in a separate pile. She could peel them, cut them up and attempt to make applesauce.

While she gathered, Gabe wandered with seeming aimlessness around the orchard. When he ambled to where she stood, stretching to pull apples from a particularly ladened branch, she stopped. She picked up one of the unmarred apples and offered it to him.

"Here," she said without emotion. "Take one."

He cocked one brow and regarded the fruit cynically.

"What's this? Are we playing Adam and Eve? You're tempting me with an apple?"

Her smile faded. She frowned and thrust the apple into his hand. "Oh, take it. You must be hungry. I wouldn't tempt you if you *were* Adam and the only man on earth."

He sighed with pretended frustration and looked down at his low-slung white shorts. "Too bad. What is it? My wardrobe? Would you like me better in a fig leaf?"

"No," Whitney snapped, angry that he could still embarrass her. Why did he say such things? He was already half-naked. Self-consciously she pulled at the knot of the pink shirt, tightening it more securely against her midriff.

"Why?" he asked. "I'd like you in fig leaves. Or not in fig leaves. I guess we wouldn't have any, would we? That came *after* eating the forbidden fruit and discovering sin."

"I don't want to talk about fig leaves," she said in disgust, turning back toward the limb of the apple tree.

"Then sit and have an apple with me," he said derisively. "Or I'll talk about them until you're crazy. Take a break. We're going to be working all day."

He was at her side, offering her one of the perfect apples. "Come on," he said, nodding at a grassy, shaded spot beneath another tree. "Take a break. It may be your last chance for a while."

She stared at the apple gleaming in his scarred and hardened hand. It was he who was tempting her, she thought, her cheeks flushed with heat. But it would be nice, wonderfully nice, to rest for a moment on the soft grass in the shade and eat something juicy and sweet.

"Come on," he said seductively, pressing the fruit into her hand. He smiled his off-center smile.

Suddenly, for no reason, she found herself smiling back. She felt a bit trembly inside. The heat and the long walk and nothing to eat, she told herself, were the cause.

He sat down in the shade, elbow propped on one bare knee. She sat beside him and bit into the apple. Even the sound of its crunch was delicious. She sighed with satisfaction and let the breeze play with the loosened tendrils of her hair.

"I like you better like that," he said, not yet eating, only watching her, his brows in a thoughtful frown.

She looked at him questioningly. Even in the shade his long, hard body seemed to glow with the sun, and his burnished hair tossed on his forehead.

"Like that," he repeated, nodding at her. "With pigtails and your shirt tied up, eating an apple. I like it a lot better than the silk suit and white blouse."

She hadn't expected compliments from him. She looked away, self-conscious again, and wriggled her toes. "With my britches tattered and my silly socks?" she asked ruefully. She looked at her feet, safely bound in the strips of his shirt.

"Yes," he said simply. "I do."

A robin warbled somewhere up in the branches of a nearby apple tree. A woodpecker made a hollow, hammering sound. Gabe bit into his apple at last, but he was still scrutinizing Whitney, his eyes narrowed.

"Did that used to be the real you?" he asked. "A girl with pigtails? One who sat in the grass eating apples?"

She pushed a strand of hair from her face. Her cheeks felt hot beneath her fingers. She didn't look at him.

"I suppose," was all she said. The scent of apples still had her half-hypnotized, and she remembered being a barefoot child at Dub's side, gathering windfall apples so that her grandmother could make them a pie. She pictured herself and Dub, munching apples on the long walk home. Once more a strange tide of homesickness overtook her.

"So what happened to that girl?" Gabe asked, lying back and leaning on his elbow. His eyes traveled up and down her body. "Where did she go and why?"

"She..." Whitney paused. She was staring out at the live oaks, but they seemed to disappear. She seemed to be looking instead across the years, watching a little girl fade into the distance. "She had to go away," she said softly. "I had to leave her by the river. When my mother came for me."

He watched her, waiting for her to go on.

She tilted her head thoughtfully and swallowed hard, remembering. "My mother always said she didn't want me to be like her. She wanted me to have an education and to be...independent. She wanted me to have everything she didn't. She used to say I was going to succeed not just for me, but for her, too."

The wind rustled in the leaves.

"You say she *came* for you," Gabe probed. "Where had she been? Where did she take you? Where had *you* been?"

She swallowed again. "Town. She'd been working in town. She took me there. I'd been with my grandmother. And my uncle. But then my mother took me. Because she got married."

He frowned. "You mean married again? To somebody besides your father?"

She stared down at her feet, wriggling her toes again, looking at the black-and-white patchwork of the makeshift bandages. Then she turned and looked him in the eye. "No," she said evenly. "It was the first time she was married. My father wouldn't marry her. He ran off and joined the army. He never came back."

Gabe said nothing for a moment. "You never saw him?" he asked at last.

"No." She nibbled at her lower lip, trying to sound calm about it all, distanced from it.

"And your stepfather?" he asked, one brow raised. His voice was low. The breeze shifted slightly, strengthening the tangy scent of ripe apples in the air.

Whitney looked away again. "My stepfather," she said from between her teeth, "was *old*. He didn't want me, really. But he wanted my mother. We tolerated each other. That was all."

He stretched out more languidly in the grass, but the intensity of his eyes belied the ease of his posture. "What about your mother? Did she love him?"

Whitney paused, wishing she'd never begun the story. She didn't even know why she was telling him, except the orchard had bewitched her, opening wide the long-shut door into her past. "No," she finally said. "She didn't love him. But he had a little money. Enough to take care of me. So she married him."

He shook his head slowly, the breeze rumpling his hair and making it glint, even in the shadows. "What happened to them?"

"He died," she said without regret. "My junior year of high school." Her tone changed and her voice choked. "She died when I was a senior in college." She clamped her lips together, still angry at the unfairness of it. Her mother had only been forty-one.

"And the others?" he asked softly. "Your grandmother? Your uncle?"

She took a deep breath. "I never saw them again," she said, blinking hard. "There was a rift—they stopped speaking to my mother because she took me away. Grandma...my grandmother died when I was still little, not long after I left her. Dub—my uncle—died a few years later.

A fishing accident. He drowned. I didn't even know for a long time. My mother wouldn't talk about him.''

There was a silence broken only by the breeze stirring the leaves of the apple trees and the occasional call of a bird.

"I'm sorry," Gabe said at last. He sounded sincere for once, not the slightest mockery in his voice.

She straightened her spine because she didn't want his pity, and she wished she'd told him nothing. Perhaps being on this island had made her a little crazy. Why else had she told him her secrets?

"Don't be sorry," she said curtly. She flung the apple core away, as far as she could. "I've done quite well for myself."

She stood up, reknotting her shirt and smoothing the loosened strands of hair back from her face.

He stayed stretched out, leaning on his elbow, looking up at her, a blade of grass clamped between his teeth. "Have you?" he asked, challenge in his voice.

"Yes," she said, "I have." She turned and walked away with her pigtails and her tattered jester's stockings.

GABE AND WHITNEY worked all afternoon to set up a second camp. They agreed it would be easiest for Mortalwood and Adrian to travel from the first site when evening started to fall and the sun stopped beating down so mercilessly.

And, once they got into the swing of their tasks, they worked together well, almost instinctively. It was, Whitney thought, both remarkable and rather eerie.

They broke pine boughs and did their best to patch the ruined roof of their new shelter. Whitney gathered moss and thickly covered the stone floor. Gabe, muscles shaking with the effort, dug another fire pit with the sharp edge of one of the flat fieldstones.

They foraged together and found the remains of the estate's dumping spot, now overgrown with weeds and brambles. Whitney, ecstatic, began to pick through the rust and rubble.

Gabe, who had started a small fire in the pit, left her to such delights and went off to look for a tidal pool in hopes of catching more mullet.

With so much to explore, Whitney was perfectly happy. Although years of rain had weathered the spot, and weeds had overrun it, she was a careful and keen-eyed scavenger. She found several unbroken jars and bottles, a bent and tarnished silver serving spoon, and best of all, an old fire-glazed earthenware crock. Its lip was chipped but the rest was intact.

"*You're* going to be cooking applesauce tonight," Whitney told the crock with satisfaction. "And I even have a spoon to stir with." She brandished the spoon as if it were a scepter and she the monarch of the island. She smiled.

Then she sat back on her heels, her smile fading. Yesterday morning, suited in silk, shod in expensive leather, she had stepped onto a yacht, thinking herself a successful, even powerful woman.

In material terms, she had everything she had ever wanted. In terms of ambition, she still had exciting worlds to conquer, and she was moving in the right circles to make such conquests. She had dismissed Gabe Cantrell as mere hired help and looked upon Mr. Mortalwood and Adrian as men of influence and great might.

Today she crouched at the edge of a dump, exulting over a chipped crock and a bent spoon. Mr. Mortalwood and Adrian were no better than invalids, and they depended on her to care for them. And she, in turn, depended on Gabe Cantrell.

The world she had to conquer was small in comparison to the sprawl of Atlanta; it was one tiny island. Her task was the oldest and simplest in the world—to survive and see that the others survived with her. For only a few days.

She looked at her hands. They were ruined, she thought with distaste. It would be weeks before they looked presentable again. As for her pierced, scratched and bandaged ankles, she didn't want to think about them. She felt hot and grimy and doubted that she'd ever feel clean again.

With her pigtails and her man's shirt and her feet in rags, she must look a fright. How people would laugh if they saw her, laugh at her as they had when she was a child. First they had laughed at her for having no father, then for having a father so old he dribbled food on his vest when he ate—

Stop it, she told herself. *Get to work. Do what needs to be done.*

She took the crock and spoon to the tiny stream and scrubbed them as furiously as she could. She was glad her mother couldn't see her now.

CHAPTER TEN

"I'M TIRED of mussels and fish," Adrian complained. He was bedraggled and crotchety after his long trek from the first camp. "Mr. M.'s right—I won't rest until I see a four-star restaurant standing here as a monument to all the sheer hell we've gone through."

Whitney ignored him and handed Mr. Mortalwood another mug of soup. Adrian had already had his ration. Gabe and Whitney had elected to go without.

Dusk was falling quickly in the grove of live oaks. Afternoon light had filtered through the leaves like gold, but now it thickened, turning a dark, misty gray.

"What day is it, Whitney? How long have we been here?" Mr. Mortalwood sat on a fallen log, huddled in his blanket. He sipped distractedly from his soup and couldn't be persuaded to eat more than a slice of steamed mullet.

Concerned, Whitney watched him closely. If the trip from the first camp had tired Adrian, it had exhausted Mr. M., even though Gabe had carried him most of the way. This morning Mr. Mortalwood had seemed physically stronger. But this evening, as night drew nearer, both his mind and body were obviously weaker.

"It's still Wednesday, Mr. M.," she said, trying to keep her voice cheerful and reassuring.

"I've fallen asleep so often I lose count," Mortalwood said querulously. "What day is it? When do the rescuers come?"

"It's Wednesday," she repeated. "They'll be here Friday. Just two more nights—it won't be bad. There's better shelter here, more water—and we have a whole apple orchard to feed us."

"If this is supposed to be applesauce, it tastes like slop," Adrian grumbled. But he kept eating, scooping the sauce out of a can with a crude spoon Gabe had carved.

"I'm sorry," Whitney snapped, her patience breaking. "I didn't have any sugar or cinnamon or raisins or butter or vanilla, Adrian. Excuse me all to pieces."

"Something sweet would be nice, Whitney," Mr. M. said almost pathetically. "The ginger ale's all gone. Do you suppose you could go back to the yacht and find more? Or some sugar perhaps? Adrian's right. This...applesauce would be better with sugar."

Whitney clamped her lips together, afraid she would make an irritable answer. She and Gabe had returned to the first camp to find Adrian and Mr. Mortalwood had drunk all four remaining cans of ginger ale and were complaining of thirst, even though they had half a jug of water left.

Whitney didn't begrudge them the drinks; she'd thought by rights and by need, Mr. M. should have had them all. But it irked her that, with so few luxuries, the two men had been so improvident. Mr. M. might still be too shaken by events to think clearly, but Adrian should have known better.

It was Gabe who spoke. He'd just wandered back from the far edge of the grove, where he'd taken his can of applesauce to eat. "We're lucky to have food at all. No. We can't go back to the boat, Mortalwood. It's dangerous. It was done the first time because you needed medicine. We have it. There won't be a second trip."

Whitney looked up at him in surprise. He'd never told her that diving for the wreck had been dangerous. She sensed tensions rising among the three men, and Adrian, with his uncombed black hair and thickening five-o'clock shadow, looked particularly ill-tempered.

"I say you go back and look again," Adrian asserted. "What's out there today that's so frightening that wasn't out there yesterday?"

Gabe didn't seem to notice Adrian's hostility. His tone calm, he went on, "We've got everything we need to survive for another two days—food, water, medicine, shelter. You're worn out, but you've got time to rest. You may be in pain, but the trick is not to give in to it."

"That's easy for you to say," Adrian bit out. "Nobody assaulted you and sprained *your* ankle. I've also been scratched to death by cactus and bitten by those damnable fire ants—"

Gabe ignored him, continuing smoothly, "People talk about tools. You know the most important? It's right here." He tapped his forefinger to his temple. "Did you hear me, Mr. Mortalwood? From here on out it's attitude that saves us and makes life bearable—nothing else. It's attitude and cooperation. You're an executive. You understand that."

Mr. Mortalwood listened with bemusement, as if the words came from very far away. But he nodded. "Yes," he said at last. "Yes."

Gabe set down his empty can and stood up tall, crossing his arms. It was a stance of quiet command. "A good executive knows how to organize manpower, how to use personnel. What this group depends on now is its survival skills. I'm the one who has them. I'd like you to put me in charge until the rescue, Mortalwood. Things will run much more smoothly."

A moment of uneasy silence followed. Whitney looked at Gabe in surprise again. She said nothing. She knew he was right, yet it rankled.

"Now wait a minute," Adrian said angrily. "Mr. Mortalwood's in no shape to make such a decision. After him, I'm the one with seniority, so I should be in charge. You—and Whitney, too—are taking advantage of my injury to seize power—"

"Power?" Whitney cried, affronted. "If you call us doing all the work while you sit around 'power,' then I suppose I have—"

Gabe interrupted her, his arms still crossed, his face unreadable in the darkening evening. "I said morale and cooperation are of the utmost importance. I meant it. Let's stop jockeying for power and assign it, once and for all. I'm nominating myself as temporary leader. I won't vote. I'll leave it to the three of you."

"I vote *against* it," Adrian practically spat. "You're a rude and unlettered man, and at some point you'll want to use this to your advantage. I won't be exploited—"

"I vote *for* Gabe," Whitney said, the strength of her own voice surprising her. "If we squabble, it only weakens us. We can only have one leader and he's obviously the best suited. I say yes."

"Oh, just like a woman, Whitney," Adrian said nastily. "You're just doing this to stab me in the back and undermine my credibility. And you've been making up to this... creature ever since we've been here. Special treatment, I suppose. Well, you've always known which side your bread was buttered on. Everyone knows *that*."

She tried to suppress the cold surge of anger rising in her. It was happening, she thought. If she gave in to her emotions now, she and Adrian would be at each other's throats. Coolly, almost regally, she ignored Adrian. "Mr. Mortalwood," she said quietly. "The deciding vote is yours. Who's to be the leader here until we're rescued? Should it be Mr. Cantrell?"

Mortalwood sat still, lost in thought, as if he hadn't been listening.

"Mr. M.?" Whitney asked softly. "Did you hear me?"

He sat in silence for a few more seconds, then made an impatient movement with his fingers, as if flicking away a troublesome insect. "Yes, yes, organization, use of personnel, delegation of authority. Certainly. Certainly, Mr. Cantrell. Yes. A wise decision. Yes."

He turned to Whitney as if seeing her for the first time. "And I expect you and Adrian to treat him with respect," he said sternly. "No complaining. An executive decision is just that—an executive decision."

"Oh, really," Adrian snarled, his tone full of venom. He rose clumsily from the log where he had sat beside Mr. M. He threw his half-filled can of applesauce across the fire pit so that it clanged and splattered against an outcropping of stone.

"You're using your wiles on him—as usual," Adrian accused Whitney. "Well, there'll be an end to *that* soon enough." He picked up the stick he was using as a cane and hobbled off by himself.

But when he reached the edge of the clearing, where the live oaks yielded to the pine woods, he stopped, as if fearful of what lay beyond.

Mr. Mortalwood stared after him dully. "Adrian," he said to Adrian's narrow back, "I told you. My decision is final. Yes, yes. Final."

Adrian looked up at the blackening sky, but kept his back turned. "Fine," he said at last. "As long as all your other decisions are final, too."

Whitney's heart took a frightened leap and a small stumble. What other decisions? What was Adrian talking about?

Mr. Mortalwood glanced at Whitney. She thought his myopic eyes looked somehow guilty. He turned his gaze from her and back toward Adrian, plucking aimlessly at the blanket draped around his shoulders. "Of course, of course," he said vaguely.

Adrian turned, and even in the dusky light, Whitney could see the look he flashed her—malicious triumph. Apprehension pierced through her.

Stunned, she turned her eyes to meet Gabe's. He looked back a long and burning moment. *I warned you,* he seemed to say.

He'd been right, she thought numbly. Adrian was contriving to stab her in the back. Perhaps he had already done it, so secretly and expertly she did not yet feel the pain.

THAT NIGHT, simply to get out of camp, she went to the bridge with Gabe to fish. Mr. Mortalwood had begged for extra sleeping pills, but she had insisted he take only his regular dosage. Soon he had fallen into a fitful doze.

Adrian, to show his superiority, wasn't speaking to either Gabe or Whitney. He sat alone on a lichen-covered rock, brooding and gazing into the fire.

The moon was full and the bridge even more awash in its light than the night before. Gabe and Whitney fished mostly in silence, with only the most superficial of conversation.

"Need help?"

"No."

"Tired? Want me to take over?"

"Thanks. Not yet."

But they were both tired, and she knew it. Even Gabe's iron constitution was showing signs of wear. She could swear that his body looked leaner than the day before.

At last they had more than a dozen mullet, enough for a fair-sized breakfast. "Let's call it a day," he said. She thought she heard weariness hiding in his voice.

She shook her head and smoothed her hair. She'd re-braided her hair before supper, but it had done no good. Somehow the wind always undid her handiwork. "Go ahead. I'll follow later," she said. "I want to take a walk on the beach. I've never seen a beach by moonlight."

In truth she wanted to be alone to think. She badly needed to sort out her thoughts and emotions.

"No," he disagreed. "It's too far for you to go back alone. Too dangerous. It was hot today. The snakes'll be out tonight. 'Gators, too."

Whitney started to protest, but he stepped toward her, laying his fingers against her lips. She started at his touch, intrigued again by the contrast between the two of them, his lean, scarred finger against the warm softness of her mouth.

"I know," he said quietly. "You're not afraid of snakes and 'gators. I'll go with you, anyway." He smiled his crooked smile. "To protect them from you."

She managed to smile back. They left the net on the bridge and the stringer hanging in a shallow bend of the river. Slowly they walked until the road gave way to the path and the path led them to the ocean.

For the past two days she had lived constantly with the unending thunder of the ocean, whether near or far away. It always seemed the same, yet it was never boring. But now, on the shore as the tide came in, the sound was truly awe-inspiring.

The beach stretched out whitely before them; there were no signs of any form of life in sight. But then, out of the corner of her eye, she saw movement.

"Oh!" cried Whitney, and without thinking she grabbed Gabe's bare arm, hugging herself to him.

Like silent, spidery phantoms, delicate creatures raced across the sand in the moonlight, so swiftly they might indeed have been enchanted. Whitney had never seen anything like them; she was not sure she was seeing them now.

"Ghost crabs," laughed Gabe. "They won't hurt you. They're more frightened of you than you are of them."

She stayed halted, watching their soundless scurry, then still unconsciously clutching Gabe's arm, she began to move on. Dozens of the small white crabs fled from them at each step, flying toward the surf or the safety or their holes.

"How eerie," she breathed. "It's like being surrounded by shy elves or something."

The sea heaved and glittered in the moonlight. The sky, full of clouds, was a complex work of silver and silvery shadow, like a composition of shifting smoke.

She looked up at Gabe, whose eyes, as usual, were on the horizon. With a swooping, tumbling feeling in her stomach, she realized how tightly she held his arm. "Oh," she said in embarrassment, releasing him. "I'm sorry."

He gave her a sideways glance and a small, lopsided smile. Her heart leapt and seemed to run away from her. If he looked like a half-naked sun god by day, he looked every inch the silver moon god at night.

"Thanks for the vote of confidence tonight," he said in a wry voice. "I wasn't sure you'd do it."

She ducked her head, watching the ghost crabs race away like fading dreams. "It had to be done," she said moodily. "Adrian's starting to crack or something. We can't go for each other's throats. It's the worst thing we could do. You're right. Attitude and cooperation are everything."

"I love it when you agree with me," he said out of the corner of his mouth. "It makes you sound so intelligent."

She gave a small, somewhat grim laugh. She paused long enough to pick up a shell. It was another sand dollar, round and perfect, with a shadowy star etched in its center.

The sea was new to her still, and she found everything about it fascinating. She slipped the pretty disk into the pocket of her slacks. She and Gabe walked on in silence for a moment.

"It won't keep," he said abruptly.

"What?" She glanced at him, puzzled.

"The sand dollar. It won't keep that way, in your pocket," he said, his eyes trained on the line where the sea met the sky. "It's too delicate. Not like a real dollar."

"Oh." She shrugged, smiling to herself. "I'll be careful."

"It's like this island," he said, nodding inland, where the pines tossed darkly. "It's...fragile. People say they'll be careful. But they usually end up ruining things. Some things aren't meant to be had. To be owned. They should stay just as nature created them."

She turned her gaze from the glistening brightness of the sea to the inland's shadowy woods. "A lecture," she said with resignation. "You're giving me a lecture, aren't you?"

"Yes," he answered.

"All this," she said, looking at the moon-whitened beach, the wheeling, enchanted clouds, "it should be left—alone, untouched."

"Yes."

"To improve it, to create an environment where lots of people can share it would be wrong, is that what you're saying?"

He stopped and stood staring down at her, his back to the moon and his face shadowy. "Did you just hear yourself?" he demanded. "*Improve* it? Who do you people think you are? Only God could improve this place. And how will you 'share' it? By destroying it with hotels and condos and marinas and golf courses?"

She took a deep breath, intending to give him a pointed and logical answer. But no words came. Only the wind and the surf spoke. With a sinking feeling she realized that she could not make an honest reply, because there was none she could make.

"Look at it," he said, more kindly than she would have expected. His rough hand touched her face, but gently. He turned it so that she had to look down the beach behind them.

The sand gleamed as white as marble, strewn here and there with small mounds of shells, a thread or two of seaweed. Their footprints trailed behind them—the prints of the only two people in the world. "You'd change *this?*" he asked, following her eyes. "You'd improve *this?*"

Slowly, shakily, she released her breath. He turned her face back to his. His hair danced like silver fire in the wind.

"What do you want me to say?" she whispered hoarsely. She couldn't betray Mr. Mortalwood's plans. She couldn't go against them now that they'd come this far and suffered this much. What did Gabe want from her?

"I don't want you to say anything," he said passionately. "I want you to *see.*"

She dropped her gaze from his in confusion and found herself staring at the outline of the alligator on his chest, dim in the moonlight.

"I can't talk about it," she said, shaking her head in perplexity. "I don't want to. I have so many things to think about. I can't think this through, too—not now."

He kept his hands against her face but didn't try to force her gaze to meet his again. "Do you know what?" he asked, intensity vibrating in his voice. "When you got on that yacht, you looked wound tighter than an overwound alarm clock. But sometimes, here, you seem almost...I don't know... 'Happy' must be the wrong word, but it's the only one I can think of. Yeah. Sometimes you've looked... happy."

He stepped a fraction of an inch closer to her. He put his other hand on her shoulder, where it seemed to burn through the fabric of her shirt. "This island has things to show you—if you'll see. It has things to tell you—if you'll hear. It has things for you to feel—if you *can* feel. And you know it. You *have* felt them. I can tell."

"No," she said, shaking her head harder, so more strands blew free and fluttered maddeningly across her eyes. "Not now. I can't talk about it now. There's too much else to be done. I'm worried about Mr. Mortalwood."

"So am I." His tone rasped with irony. "In more ways than one."

"And Adrian's up to something," she said, trying to push her hair from her face. "That's all too clear."

His hand fell from her jaw and gripped her other shoulder. "I warned you about him. He's your enemy. And I don't trust Mortalwood, either—he's a weak man, Whitney."

"Oh, don't be impossible," she protested, her mouth twisting with unhappiness. "Poor Mr. M.—he isn't himself. He seemed better this morning, but tonight I'm scared. He...what if...if anything happened? It'd be my fault, my..."

He shook her lightly to make her aware of how wild she was beginning to sound. "Frankly it scares me, too," he said. "But if he gets any worse, I'll take care of it, I promise you."

"Take care?" she protested. "How? What can you do that we haven't already done? What's left?"

He took her face between his hands. "I'll do whatever has to be done. I promise you that. I promise."

"And you," she said vehemently, beginning to lose control of all her conflicting emotions. "Why didn't you tell me that diving for that wreck was dangerous? Why didn't you *tell* me? What's dangerous about it? Don't keep things from me. Not ever. *Don't.*"

"All wrecks are dangerous," he said, trying to tilt her face so she looked into his eyes. "The ocean depths are dangerous. There are sharks. Manta rays. Jellyfish. I did it once, but I don't feel like doing it twice. Not for ginger ale, for God's sake. Not while you're here to take care of."

"You *don't* take care of me," she said. She stamped her foot, a childish gesture she hadn't made in years. "I take care of myself."

"Shhh," he soothed. "Don't get excited. You're right. We'll talk about it later. Shhh. Be good, and I'll give you a present. I have something for you."

"A present," she said, twisting away from him miserably. "I don't want a present. Don't treat me like a...a child."

"It's not a child's present," he said. He stepped close behind her, putting one hand on her upper arm. His voice was soft in her ear. "It's for a woman."

"I don't want it," she said, staring out at the spangled sea. His touch made her tremble, and she willed herself to be still. She willed it so much that she trembled even more.

"Wait till you see it," he said, and taking her hand, he slipped something plastic into it and then closed his fingers over the object. She could feel his breath against the back of her neck, tickling and teasing and tingling.

She looked at the small object he had given her. She blinked with surprise. She turned to face him, half in astonishment, half in irritation. "Dish-washing soap?" she demanded. "Are you crazy? We hardly have any dishes. Is this your idea of a woman's gift?"

He laughed low, deep in his throat. "Whitney, read the label. It's biodegradable. You can wash your hair with it. Bathe with it. In the sea. It's good for you and it won't hurt the sea."

"What?" she asked, not quite comprehending. She stared at the bottle again.

"We've had a long, hot day," he said. He knelt at her feet and slipped off her right sandal. He began to unwind the strips of his shirt from her leg and foot.

"What are you doing?" she asked, nervous at his touch. Her blood seemed to ebb and flow in a phantom imitation of the moon-bright sea.

"Taking off your silly-socks so we can get into the ocean." He slipped off her other sandal and began to unwind the fabric from that foot. He put the pile of strips beneath a rock to weight them down.

"Come on." He stood and held out his hand to her. "Let's both cool off."

"But you said . . ." she protested, drawing back.

"We'll stay in the shallow water," he promised, "where the monsters are afraid to come."

"But . . ." she began again, worrying about sharks and jellyfish.

"Trust me," he said. He took her by the hand and led her down the beach toward the water.

At first she was frightened, but the water felt so wonderfully cool she stopped worrying and simply lost herself in its delicious embrace. She wet her hair and he helped her work the soap into it before she rinsed it clean again. She had to admit that, after the long, hot day, it was wonderful, and she felt as clean as if she'd been reborn into a spotless new body.

He poured a few drops of soap into his hand and smoothed it, bubbling, over the back and shoulders and arms of her wet shirt. "Oh," she sighed, as a wave splashed her, washing part of the suds away. "That feels divine. Oh, it's wonderful. Don't stop. Don't ever stop."

"Somehow," he said wryly, "I'd always hoped you'd say that. But not while I was rinsing you out like a pair of socks."

She laughed, feeling for a magical instant renewed and refreshed.

He walked her to even shallower water, where the cresting waves reached only to her knees. The chill of the water left her feeling suddenly sapped of strength, but still happy. His arm was around her waist, and he drew her nearer.

She looked up into his eyes, then at his chest, smiling. She felt intoxicated by moonlight and seawater and cleanness and fatigue. "What *is* this?" she asked shyly, laying her forefinger against the tattoo on his chest. "Why do you have an alligator on you?"

He laughed and put both his hands on her waist. "Remember when it was the required fashion for the male of the species to wear one of those shirts with the little alligator on the chest?"

She nodded, still tracing it with her forefinger. She remembered the shirts. They had all been the rage once.

"Well," he said, raising a brow in derision, "I had this girlfriend who didn't think I was...stylish. She kept nagging me to get a shirt with an alligator. I didn't want to. She kept nagging, so I thought, if she wants an alligator on my chest, I'll bloody well give her an alligator on my chest."

She laughed and laid her head against his damp shoulder. "That's so like you," she said, nuzzling him fondly. "So absolutely like you. What did she think?"

"She hated it. She never spoke to me again," he said, wrapping his arms around her, shielding her from the sweep of the wind, which was cold against her wet flesh.

She found that her hands were resting on the hard, smooth skin of his shoulders. She drew back to look up into his face. The sea twinkled and danced behind him, and the moonlight spilled down on his even features.

"I said it was like you," she mused, her words coming slowly, "but I don't know you. I know nothing about you. Not really. Who are you?" she asked, searching his face. "You've never told me. *What* are you?"

He bent his head to hers and gave her a brief kiss on the lips that was almost brotherly.

"I'm your friend," he said, drawing back, his voice low. He smoothed her wet hair. "As long as we're on this island, I'm your friend. Remember that."

Something in his voice made all the playfulness and trust drain from her. "But when we're off the island?" she asked. The wind rose, making her shudder.

"Off the island, I may be something else," he said. "It depends."

"Do you mean you could be an enemy?" she asked, and shuddered again.

He stared down at her for a long moment. "Yes," he said.

The single word chilled her more than the wind. *I don't want you to be my enemy,* she thought with a sickening shock of realization. *I think I could love you.*

But she couldn't love him, she told herself, now shivering uncontrollably. She didn't know anything about him—except that she could trust him with her life.

"How...how much of an enemy?" she asked, her voice shaking.

"I don't know," he said tensely, pulling her nearer to him. "Maybe worse than Fisk. Or Mortalwood—in his way. Maybe the worst you've ever had."

He bent and kissed her again. This time there was nothing brotherly in it. There was all the passion of a man dangerously poised between playing lover and enemy.

The moon tugged at the tide and the tide tugged at them, trying to sweep them away.

CHAPTER ELEVEN

FOR A MOMENT Whitney lost herself in the wild, dark universe of his kiss. She barely felt the strong surge and ebb of the waves around her ankles. The wind blew in her hair, drying and tangling it, but she didn't notice.

She could only cling to Gabe, her eyes tightly shut, the sound of the sea pounding in her ears. Her fatigue fell away, and the thousand fears, large and small, that had harried her mercifully disappeared. It might be wrong to want him so. Paradoxically it might be right, perhaps the only right thing.

Darkness and touch and yearning; the world turned to these primal things and became simple and exciting again, not terrifying. There was no weakness because Gabe was there with all his strength. There was no loneliness because he was there with all his warmth.

But then he drew away. "Well," he said wryly, "that felt like it could lead to something. I'll have that much to look back on, at least." He took her chin in his hand, "Whitney, Whitney." He shook his head helplessly. "I'm not who you think. Or what you think. Hell, I have to say this. I *am* the enemy. I came to try to save all this—to save it from you."

He gestured down the shining beach where the waves foamed like silvery fire. She looked around them blindly, not understanding, then back up at him.

"Save it?" she whispered, stepping back from his touch. She no longer felt warmth or strength issuing from him.

Betrayal was what radiated from him now, deep and sickening.

"I know what you're up to," he said.

She jerked her face away from his touch. For a moment she thought he was going to reach for her, but he didn't.

"We suspected from the start," he said harshly. "That's why the owner of the marina asked me to captain the yacht, to keep my eyes open, learn what I could."

A spy, Whitney thought dully. The thought hit her as hard as a blow, making her almost physically ill. She turned from him in heartsick rage and began wading wildly toward shore.

It was a long walk, and the water no longer felt cooling. Instead it seemed to numb and shrivel her. Dimly she heard splashing and knew Gabe was keeping pace beside her. She tried to move faster, to escape him and the pain he had inflicted on her.

A spy. Deceiving all of them, stealing their secrets, playing with her emotions. What else had he done to them? she wondered angrily. What else would he do? And whom did he represent? It might easily be the worst sort of people.

"Just whom," she asked, darting him a poisonous look, "are you spying *for?* Some radical save-the-Earth survivalist group? Did you wreck us here purposely—to punish us? I've heard some of you won't stop at anything—not even violence. Well, if anything happens to Mr. M.—"

He stopped, his arm snaking out and seizing her by the wrist. "I'm trying to be truthful," he said angrily. "Don't start calling names and hurling accusations until you hear—"

"Did you?" she demanded, furious. "Did you sink that boat? If you did—"

"No." The word rang out like a shot on the air, and he tightened his grip on her wrist. She curled her lip to show him he didn't frighten her. "Now, listen," he ordered, yanking her closer. "I'm not a violent man."

"Then what do you call this?" she asked in triumph, nodding down at the hand clamped almost painfully on her wrist.

He made a sound of disgust and released her, as if touching her had become a repulsive act.

"I didn't touch that damned boat. Mortalwood neglected her. And she turned out to be in worse shape than she looked."

"So," Whitney said, walking toward shore again, shaking her hair from her eyes, "the poor corporate spy got caught here along with the rest of us. With nothing to do but spy some more. I hope it's been a fruitful trip," she said with all the sarcasm she could muster.

"Fruitful enough," he said, his voice icy calm. "I can figure it out. Mrs. Fredericks owns this island. She's always intended to leave it to the public as a protected wilderness area. Somebody's talking her into thinking about selling. That somebody can only be her son. How am I doing so far?" he asked maliciously.

Whitney didn't answer. She'd reached the shore, where she headed for a piece of driftwood and sat down. She had to wind those damnable strips of rag around her feet again or be pierced and scratched by all the cacti hiding in the dark.

He stood and watched her struggle with the makeshift bandages. This time he made no offer to help. "Mrs. Fredericks is getting old," Gabe said, mockery and venom lacing his tone. "Her son, by all accounts, has never amounted to much. But maybe he's been able to talk his mother into selling the island to a private business interest. Like yours. Like the Mortalwood Corporation."

Furiously Whitney worked to twist and knot the rags into some crude protection, but she was so angry that her hands shook. She simply couldn't perform the task.

Gabe knelt in front of her and took over. When she started to protest, he told her, with false amiability, to shut up or walk all the way back on cactus. She sat stiff and resentful while his sure hands wound the strips around her legs.

"So..." he said, not looking at her, concentrating on his work. "So I ask myself what Sheldon Fredericks gets out of this—out of his mother's selling the island. Money? Eventually, yes. But what does he get immediately? The best possible answer is *power*. Your friend Fisk has been working with Sheldon Fredericks to arrange a trade-off. The company gets the island. But Sheldon gets power in the company. After all these years, the worthless fool's a success. He'll have an excellent job. Probably yours."

Expertly he tied the last knot, and at that moment she stood, anxious to be away from him. "You don't know what you're talking about," she said hotly. "Mr. Mortalwood would never...never sell me out. You're crazy."

She wheeled away and left him kneeling there, a taunting smile on his face. Then she heard the crunch of sand and knew he was right behind her, following.

She kept her head down, watching her path with every ounce of her concentration. She didn't want to think about what Gabe had said. It made too much sense in a horrible, nauseating way.

Mr. Mortalwood *had* spoken of using stock to buy the island. How much stock? Enough to give Fredericks considerable control? Enough to let Fredericks choose among the company's best positions for himself?

She had worked hard at her job, furiously at it. She considered Mr. Mortalwood as much a friend as an employer. He wouldn't hold her back so that Sheldon Fredericks could advance with no qualification other than his wealth—and this island. He wouldn't. Mr. M. was an honorable man, a civilized man.

She was breathing hard by the time she reached the bridge. Gabe caught up with her, strolling easily by her side. The corona of his hair stirred in the wind, and moonlight silvered his nearly naked body.

Savage, she thought uncharitably. *Stone savage.*

"How'd I get mixed up in this?" he asked, even though she had been pointedly ignoring him. "I'm a small part of an outfit called the Wilderness Conservancy. We raise funds to buy endangered areas or go to court to protect them."

"Ugh," she said with simple eloquence. There were dozens of environmental groups. A few of them weren't above threats, sabotage and thuggery. She had no soft spot for them.

"The Wilderness Conservancy keeps quiet, does things peacefully, and it moves through the proper channels," he said. "I belong to it. So do a lot of people. Including Clark, the man who owns the marina. Mortalwood called him, asking for a captain with no local ties. Clark was suspicious. There'd been whispers about the island. I'm new in town. Hardly anybody knows me. Clark asked me to captain. And keep a sharp eye."

"How thrilling," Whitney snapped. "But next time you want information, just question me at gunpoint, all right? It's faster, more direct—more *honest,* if you can understand what that means."

"Look," he said, anger resonating in his voice again, "twenty years ago, this was described as one of the three finest unspoiled Atlantic seashore areas. It's worth protecting. And I've got my own interest in it—"

"I'm sure you do," she said coldly. "Most people talk a good game of ideals, but—in the end—they always have their 'own interests.' Always. Do I expect you to be different? No."

"I believe in the importance of wilderness," he said from between his teeth. "People need it. It feeds the soul the way manmade things never can. We're all creatures of nature. But ninety-nine percent of the time we forget.''

''I wish I could forget it myself,'' Whitney shot back, moving into the shadows of the pine grove. ''I wish I were going to a hotel room with a Jacuzzi and a pound of chocolates. I'd fall on my knees and kiss the manmade carpet.''

''Maybe you would,'' he said contemptuously, ''but not everybody feels that way. Some people want to come home to the wilderness. I take them. That's my job. I run wilderness expeditions.''

''Home?'' She laughed, then swore as she stubbed her toe in the darkness. ''People want to come home to this? Ha!''

Once more he reached out and took her arm, stopping her. Even in the shadow of the pines she could see how he narrowed his eyes as he bent above her. ''I had a wilderness-vacation company in Oregon,'' he said. ''I liked it. Teaching people how to get back to basics. I was good at it. So good I decided to relocate and expand. Here, centered in Georgia. We're talking a half-million-dollar operation. Where I have access to these islands and the Everglades, Okefenokee, and someday even the rain forest.''

She took a deep breath as she pushed his hand away from hers. ''Don't touch me. Don't tell me your life story. I'm not interested. But don't worry—I'll keep your dirty little secrets till we're off this island. I don't want to upset Mr. Mortalwood. And someday, when all this is over, I want to come back and dance on what *used* to be your precious wilderness. I hope it's all paved over, every inch of it, and I'll dance on it.''

''My God,'' he said, shaking his head in wonder. ''My God, but you're a little savage. And a shortsighted fool. Maybe Mortalwood deserves you—and you deserve him.''

They were almost at the edge of the grove of live oaks. ''Go on,'' he said, his voice low. ''You can make it from here, I suppose. Go back to them. Your own kind.''

He turned and left her standing in the shadows, her heart pounding.

MR. MORTALWOOD was awake and restless. He must have heard her come back to the camp, for he stirred and called her name. His bed of moss rustled.

"Yes?" She stared up at the moonlight pouring through the trees, silvering the Spanish moss as it swayed in the breeze.

"I can't sleep. Give me another pill—please."

She sighed, not knowing whether to let him chance spending a sleepless night. Adrian snored soundly beside him, so soundly that Whitney suspected he might have helped himself to a couple of Mr. M.'s pills.

"I don't think you should," she said. The moon-washed grove was so ancient, so peaceful, so majestic, she thought. Why did they have to come to it dragging so many complicated problems? In the distance the surf boomed.

"Whitney—" Mr. Mortalwood's voice was quavery and entreating "—come sit by me. If you won't give me a pill...sit by me. Talk to me."

She sighed again, knowing it was best to indulge him. She went and settled cross-legged next to him. She adjusted his blanket.

Where's Gabe? she wondered. *Out on that moonlit beach somewhere?*

And what, she wondered, would he do to thwart Mr. Mortalwood's plans when they got back to the mainland? The wilderness was his passion. It was also his job. What forces would he set loose like hounds on the Mortalwood Corporation and on Mrs. Fredericks? Media, pressure groups, lawyers, lobbyists, people of influence? All of those, she supposed wearily.

"Whitney?" Mortalwood's voice sounded even more unsure than before. He hesitated. "Would you mind holding my hand again?"

Her apprehensions flared like a flame fed by wind. "No, Mr. M.," she said as kindly as she could. "I don't think that's a good idea, either."

"Please," he said. "I have to talk to you. I...I have to. It'll be easier if I hold your hand. Please."

She took a deep breath of the clean night air. She remembered Gabe's warning all too well and wished she were alone somewhere, the empty beach, the windswept bridge, anywhere. "No," she repeated. "I don't think so. Let's just talk."

But he said nothing. The leaves whispered, the insects clicked and hummed, the surf droned in the distance. Whitney drew up her knees, put her arms around them and lay her forehead tiredly against them.

It would all be so peaceful and lovely here, she thought, *if only there were no people. It's the kind of place where I could put my mind and soul back together—if only there were no people.*

"Whitney, my dear," he said at last in a low voice, "to get the island, I have to trade some stock—and let Sheldon Fredericks become executive vice president. And eventually CEO. He'll want Adrian under him, not you."

She didn't move, didn't so much as flinch. She kept sitting with her forehead hidden against her knees. The most surprising thing, she thought with irony, is that she wasn't surprised.

"It's for the good of the corporation," Mortalwood said with an attempt at firmness, but he sounded guilty, a bit unsure of himself. "It's one of the things we wanted to talk to you about at Hilton Head. At the end, after other matters were discussed. Adrian thought it best that way."

Whitney squeezed her eyes tightly shut. So Adrian had done it. He had outmaneuvered her, undone her, worked behind her back.

"But we planned to make it up to you," Mortalwood added hastily. "Oh, dear, this is difficult. But in light of all you've done . . . I thought I should be honest. You see, you won't actually lose anything, Whitney. What we have in mind is a lateral promotion. To create a new title and put you in charge of public relations—with a substantial raise in pay, of course."

Opening her eyes, she raised her face and looked up through the opening of the shelter at the stars. How bright they were. One never saw stars that bright in the city or town. Only in places like this.

"Mr. M.," she said quietly, "I don't want a lateral promotion. That really means no promotion at all, and we both know it. And I don't want public relations. My specialty is management. Money's nice, but I'm not in it for the money. It's my *career.*"

Besides, she thought bitterly, public relations would be a hotbed of problems once the news was out that they intended to buy the island. No wonder Adrian wanted her in charge; it would be the most unpleasant and volatile job in the company. It was a job designed to make her enemies, and chief among those enemies would be Gabe.

"But," he said defensively, "the corporation *is* your career. What's best for the corporation is best for you—" A coughing fit seized him. Whitney poured him a cup of water and held it to his lips. He drank, stopped coughing and managed to capture one of her hands in his. In spite of herself, she winced at his touch.

"I knew you'd be disappointed at first," Mr. Mortalwood said. A touch of desperation edged his voice. "I'd never willingly hurt you. I know how much you meant to Lila—you were like the daughter we'd never had—but this is business you see, and I must do what's best for the company. *You* must do what's best for the company. You've shown on this wretched island that you can rise to a challenge. Now I'm offering you the biggest challenge of all—dealing with the public relations of this deal, defending our image, fighting those cursed environmentalists. Oh, they'll want my head on a stake, Whitney, but you...you can save me. Save the company, save all of us...."

Whitney could not bear to listen to more. For the second time that night, she felt betrayed, deceived, used and manipulated. For years she had been loyal to Mr. Mortalwood and his corporation. She had poured all her energy into his and Lila's enterprises, and while Lila was alive, she had been treated fairly. Now Lila was gone, and Whitney's only reward was underhandedness and treachery.

Dropping Mr. Mortalwood's hand, she rose swiftly from his side and fled. "Whitney?" he called after her. "You'll understand. Really you will...."

But she didn't turn back to him. She ran down the path until, her breath coming in torn gasps, she reached the sands of the shore again.

The moon sparkled on the water, and the sound of the surf filled her ears, drumming as loudly as her heart.

The beach was empty, almost spectral. As far as she could see, no other human being moved. The ghost crabs fled at her approach, vanishing like creatures made of mist.

She was alone with the moon and the sand and the sea. And she was alone with herself, too, as alone as she had ever been in her life.

That suddenly seemed very lonely indeed.

CHAPTER TWELVE

AND THEN, the next morning, it was all over. Rescue arrived in the form of a large pleasure boat whose keen-eyed owner had seen a ribbon of smoke rising from the woods. He was one of the few people who knew that no campers would be on the island until Friday.

Gabe saw him make course for the island, and he met him at the weathered dock, telling him to radio the mainland and have an ambulance waiting; two of the party needed medical attention.

The voyage back should have seemed like traveling first-class to heaven to Whitney. The boat had a small head where she washed her face and hands and body with real soap and dried with a real towel. She was given a partial change of clothes, a T-shirt a bit too large, but clean and dry and free of sand.

The boat had a small galley where the owner's wife made them real coffee and thick ham sandwiches with mayonnaise and lettuce and fresh tomato slices. And, perhaps most importantly, the boat had speed. Once more the island became a speck in the distance, and then it disappeared.

The trip to the mainland shore was, however, anything but heavenly. Adrian was speaking to neither Gabe nor Whitney. Whitney could barely look Mr. Mortalwood in the face, and he, in turn, seemed embarrassed, defensive and tongue-tied in her presence. She ignored Gabe, and Gabe ignored her.

When they drew near the dock on the coast, an ambulance waited, gleaming whitely in the sun. Whitney supposed she should accompany the two men to the hospital to make sure both were all right. After that, she had only the vaguest idea of where she would go or what she would do or how she would get back to Atlanta.

She heard Gabe ask the skipper of their rescue boat to lend him a few dollars' worth of change. Her heart contracted. She knew the money was for phone calls. He would step off the boat and never look back. He would not wait one instant before reporting what he knew about them.

He would phone the media, the Wilderness Conservancy, perhaps members of the Fredericks family itself. What he had warned her about was true: he had become the enemy. He and his sort would fight her and the Mortalwood Corporation for the island, and they would fight till the end of their strength.

When the boat was safely moored, she saw that she was right. Gabe shook hands with the owner and his wife. Then he kicked off Mr. Mortalwood's scuffed white shoes and walked away barefoot, like some wild, free prince.

He did not so much as nod to Whitney or the others. He walked away and, as she'd expected, didn't look back. He disappeared almost immediately into a building that seemed as if it might have a phone. The only sign he had ever existed at all were the empty shoes standing on the deck. But looking at those empty shoes, Whitney knew, sick at heart, the battle for Sand Dollar had begun.

But she hardly had time to think about that. She found herself frantically explaining Mr. Mortalwood's current problems and his medical background to the ambulance attendants, giving them his medication, assuring him that he was safe at last and would be fine.

She should have felt a sense of deliverance. Instead she felt a deadening emptiness, as if the most important part of herself had been left, forsaken, on the island.

The island itself seemed vague and dreamlike now, and all the events that had taken place on it seemed something that could not have possibly happened to her. As she walked next to Mr. Mortalwood's gurney as it was wheeled to the ambulance, she moodily thrust her hand into her pocket, feeling for the shells she'd picked up.

The smooth little olive shell was there intact. It assured her that she really had been cast away. But the sand dollar was gone. Actually it was not that it had disappeared, it had dissolved. No longer a delicate marvel, it had turned to grit and dust and rubble in her pocket.

When she drew the fragments out, they sifted through her fingers and were carried away by the wind.

ALTHOUGH WHITNEY FOUGHT against admitting it, there was nothing for her to do in the end, of course, but leave the corporation. She knew it was her only course of action, but at first she tried to avoid the truth, for it was painful. Mr. Mortalwood tried everything to have his way, yet keep her happy: he rationalized, pleaded, offered her more money, promised to create a new position for her, executive vice president in charge of public relations. At last he was reduced to sentimental appeals to her memory of Lila.

Saddened, Whitney knew none of this could hold her in the corporation any longer, not even the gratitude she felt toward Lila. She supposed that from Mr. Mortalwood's point of view, he hadn't actually conspired with Adrian against her. Still, she couldn't help feeling betrayed.

She had never trusted Adrian. Now she found that she couldn't trust Mr. M.'s judgment or his fairness, either, not when he didn't have Lila at his side, guiding him.

But ultimately, what drove the final wedge between Whitney and Mr. Mortalwood and made the split complete was the matter of the island.

Gabe had moved as swiftly as Whitney had feared, breaking the story of the sale of Sand Dollar for developmental purposes to the Mortalwood Corporation. The media howled and bayed when they heard the news. Every environmental group on the Atlantic coast showed its teeth in challenge. So did groups inland. Citizens ranted. The mildest public reaction was disgust, pure and simple.

Finally Whitney had walked into Mr. M.'s office, thrown the editorial pages of *The Atlanta Constitution* on his desk and said without preamble, "They're right." He looked up at her in surprise.

"They're right," she repeated stiffly. "You'd be foolish to touch that island. It'll cost you your reputation. People will despise you. Who knows? You might even come to despise yourself."

He had stared at her with resentful disbelief.

"Besides," she said when he didn't reply, "it's *wrong*. It's just flat wrong to take something that beautiful and to…to rape it. Almost all the other islands have been commercialized. Leave this one. So people and their children and their children's children can see what nature created. It's part of our heritage. Don't despoil it."

"Whitney," he had said soberly, distaste pulling down the corners of his mouth, "are you mad? I keep telling you—this is business. Of all people, I'd expect you to understand that."

"It's bad business," she returned. "If you go on with it, I'll quit."

They stared at each other for a long moment, and she knew then that something was ending forever. A part of her life was over. "I'm sorry," she said finally. "I'll always be grateful to you. But it's time for me to move on. I can't be part of this.''

SHE SOLD HER Mercedes, moved to a cheaper apartment and set up a small management-consulting agency in downtown Atlanta, then prepared for a long stretch of unemployment. It arrived immediately and lay down like a hungry wolf at her door. The phone in her little office seldom rang. Few people knocked at her door. She set her jaw and counted on her savings and determination to survive.

Slowly business came. A company that marketed onions consulted her. So did a small mail-order firm specializing in peach preserves. And then a fledgling tour group and a neighborhood mini-mall.

It was gratifying to see success slowly building, but it was also surprisingly lonely. Whitney had always been a team player, had enjoyed being part of a company. Now she *was* the company. It felt odd to her, satisfying, but not quite complete.

In the meantime, while Whitney struggled, public outcry against the development of the island had been so great that Mrs. Fredericks decided against selling. After the uproar had gone on for five months, she once again declared her intention to leave it as a protected wilderness area with restricted public use. The day that Whitney heard the announcement was the only time since she'd left the island that she'd felt real happiness, and at the same time, paradoxically, the only time she'd felt a choking sensation in her throat and the sting of tears.

At least some good came out of all this mess, she thought. *The most important thing was saved. The island would stay as it was, untouched, lonely and quietly majestic.*

She now realized how important its protection was. She had revisited it a hundred times in her mind, walked the empty beach again, strolled among the live oaks and pines.

stood on the moonlit bridge. The place stayed in her memory like a strange and wonderful gift that nature had bestowed. Mentally she visited it in times of stress, and always it restored her.

She would have liked to look up Gabe and tell him. But she didn't. It might seem like weakness, and she was Whitney Shane, an extremely strong woman. But she missed him. She missed him so terribly she couldn't bring herself to admit how much. She tried to throw herself into her work to forget him. So far, she hadn't succeeded.

One day a few weeks after Mrs. Fredericks's announcement that the island was again safe, a bold rap jarred Whitney's office door.

She looked up blearily from a page of statistics. What now? Was the president of the onion company showing up early this week? She hoped not. The man was obsessed with onions; he could talk of onions and onions only. Nothing fascinated him more than endless discussions of the management of the onion industry.

She'd pored over so many dry statistics lately she wondered if she needed glasses. Rubbing her eyes, she went to the door and opened it.

A handsome blond man in clean jeans and a khaki safari shirt stepped in. He had a neatly trimmed dark gold beard, and he smelled of old-fashioned after-shave.

For a moment she didn't recognize him. He looked too neat, too tailored, far too civilized. Then the shock of recognition struck.

Gabe, she thought, and her body turned to fire and ice at the same moment. She stared up at him wordlessly, emotions whirling. What was he doing in Atlanta? She could not imagine, and could not find her voice to ask the question.

"Hello," he said.

She still could not speak.

He frowned slightly, looking first around the small office, then taking in Whitney. She wore a simple suit of navy blue, one of her businesslike white blouses, and had her hair swept back into a simple French twist.

"I hear you've gone independent. Into management consulting," he said.

"Yes," she answered, her voice thick. He looked wonderful, she thought. And he looked successful. She had read about his company, Wild Places, Inc., in the business pages of the newspaper. It was thriving. People were hungry to get back to nature. Now, after the island, she understood why. Such places, such experiences, could change people, change them profoundly. "It seems you're doing well with your business," she managed.

He cast his eyes around the immaculate office again. "Yes," he said with a shrug, "but I'm not sure I can manage—alone. I might need a partner."

She blinked in surprise. "Partner?"

Suddenly he didn't look quite as confident. He shifted his weight and looked out her single window. "Partner," he said, and nodded, not looking at her. "Somebody willing to take chances. Somebody willing to work hard, to build—and to share things fifty-fifty."

"I see," she said, but she didn't. She touched the glass top of her desk nervously, running well-manicured fingernails along its smoothness.

He continued to stare out the window as if something fascinating lay beyond it. In truth, her window offered little in the way of a view, so she couldn't imagine what it was he saw. But then he was always looking out toward some horizon. It was his nature.

"What I have in mind is a woman of exceptional qualities," he said, his voice low. "Courage. Brains. The ability to appreciate beauty. And integrity. That's always hardest to find. She's got to have integrity. Stick up for what's right." He paused. "And she'd have to be forgiving." He sighed harshly. "Very forgiving."

He turned, and his gray eyes met her blue ones, jolting through her like lightning. "I heard you left him. Left them all. Mortalwood. Walked out. I hadn't expected that."

She bit the corner of her lip and nodded. She supposed word had gotten around. She was surprised it had gotten as far as Savannah, where he was based.

He shrugged and stared out the window again. "Well, I misjudged you. You were so kind to the fool, I thought... Well, it wasn't fair what I thought. I apologize."

Whitney drew a shaky breath and bit her lip harder.

He shook his head and frowned. "I apologize—I came to tell you that. And to ask you for something. Will you accept the apology? And will you listen?"

When she didn't reply, he turned to look at her again. When she nodded, his eyes met hers and held them. "This is hard to say, Whitney," he said. "I'm good at part of what I do, but there are... skills I lack. I'm good in the field, organizing expeditions, leading them, training new leaders. But other things—keeping books, checking orders, making the whole thing run right... I can do it. But I don't *like* it."

He looked at her again, and something in his look made a frisson of happiness run through her. "You're good at all those things. I heard you were available," he said. "So I thought of you."

"Oh," was all she could say. She remembered him with the sun and wind in his hair. She remembered him silvered with moonlight.

He moved nearer. His voice grew more intent. "Once I started thinking about you, I couldn't stop."

He stood close enough to touch her. Silence seemed to overwhelm them both. She glanced away from him, fiddled with the button at her blouse collar.

"But Whitney," he breathed, "I couldn't live with just any partner. I told you. She has to have everything I said—and more. She can't be afraid of mud or alligators or anything else. She'd have to be able to cast a fishnet. And track raccoons."

She smiled uneasily and tugged at her lapel, straightening it.

"The tricky part," he said, his voice slow, a bit hesitant, "is she'd have to love me. At least a little bit as much as I love her. Could she? Would she?"

She was filled with too much confusion and tumult to answer coherently. She began to button up her jacket, a nervous movement, but suddenly his hand was on hers.

"No," he said, a surprising beseechment in his voice, "please, Whitney. Don't button up and shut me out."

They stared into each other's eyes. Slowly his hands moved to the lapels of her jacket and he began to draw it from her shoulders. "Please," he repeated, gently stripping it from her. "Don't button up against me and shut me out. I couldn't stand it."

He lay the jacket on her desk and reached up to touch her hair. "Please," he said for the third time. "Oh, Whitney, it's like at the island. I'm at your feet, as usual, just in a different way this time."

Whitney again fingered the button at her collar and, as she lost herself in his eyes, undid it. She took another deep breath, as if loosening the button had let her breathe freely for the first time in her life.

"Can you?" he asked, taking her face between his hands. "Do you think you could manage? To do all that? And to love me? I swear, I believed old Mortalwood would convince you he needed you, or worse that he'd tell you he'd fallen in love with you. How could he help it, I thought, when *I'd* done it so fast? Will you come with me?"

She felt him loosening her hair, felt it spilling over her shoulders. Suddenly she felt as if they were no longer caught in the confines of a tiny office crammed into the city's most hectic business section.

She felt as if they were alone in a wonderful, unexplored place, wide and wild and free. She could almost feel the wind in her hair, the sand beneath her feet, hear the steady thunder of the waves.

Suddenly she knew that she loved this man and what he stood for. It was as if the long-separated parts of herself had come together and were whole at last.

"I could manage," she said as he lowered his lips to hers. "Oh, yes, I could manage."

As they kissed, he laced his hands through her tumbled hair. "I love you," he said against her lips. "I love the executive and the woman and the scared little tomboy of a kid. I love them all."

"Yes, yes," she whispered back. "They all love you, too. *I* love you, Gabe. It could only be you."

SOMEWHERE FAR AWAY the surf tumbled a sand dollar onto a deserted shore. It lay whole and perfect and shining in the sun. It belonged to no one. It belonged to everyone. Beyond it lay the sea, and above it stretched a sky where gulls wheeled, free as the wind itself.

HARLEQUIN
Romance®

**HARLEQUIN ROMANCE
IS BETTING ON LOVE!**

And The Bridal Collection's
September title is a sure bet.

**JACK OF HEARTS (#3218)
by Heather Allison**

THE BRIDAL
COLLECTION

THE BRIDE played her part.
THE GROOM played for keeps.
THEIR WEDDING was in the cards!

Available in August in
THE BRIDAL COLLECTION:

THE BEST-MADE PLANS (#3214)
by Leigh Michaels

Harlequin Romance

Wherever Harlequin
books are sold.

WELCOME TO

The quintessential small town, where everyone knows everybody else!

Finally, books that capture the pleasure of tuning in to your favorite TV show!

GREAT READING...GREAT SAVINGS...AND A FABULOUS FREE GIFT!

Each book set in Tyler is a self-contained love story; together, the twelve novels stitch the fabric of the community. The covers honor the old American tradition of quilting; each cover depicts a patch of the large Tyler quilt.

With Tyler you can receive a fabulous gift, ABSOLUTELY FREE, by collecting proofs-of-purchase found in each Tyler book. And use our special Tyler coupons to save on your next TYLER book purchase.

Join your friends at Tyler for the seventh book, ARROWPOINT by Suzanne Ellison,
available in September.

Rumors fly about the death at the old lodge! What happens when Renata Meyer finds an ancient Indian sitting cross-legged on her lawn?
